CITY GIRL IN THE OUTBACK

ALLY BLAKE

ROMANCE

Recycling programs for this product may not exist in your area.

ISBN-13: 978-1-335-21701-1

City Girl in the Outback

For questions and comments about the quality of this book, please contact us at CustomerService@Harlequin.com.

Harlequin Enterprises ULC
22 Adelaide St. West, 41st Floor
Toronto, Ontario M5H 4E3, Canada
www.Harlequin.com

HarperCollins Publishers
Macken House, 39/40 Mayor Street Upper,
Dublin 1, D01 C9W8, Ireland
www.HarperCollins.com

Printed in U.S.A.

1 2 3 4 5 6 7 8 9 10 HDC 28 27 26 25

A dazzling, brand-new quartet from Harlequin Romance!

Outback Kings

Four heirs... A one-billion-dollar legacy!

In Australia's remote northwest lies the Kimberley, home to the nation's largest cattle station—Kings Reach. From there tycoon rancher Fraser King runs a billion-dollar dynasty. It's his job to protect the family legacy and he has plans none of his four sons saw coming...

Returning home for a lavish ball honoring their late mother, Tom, Fitz, Logan and Jack are reunited. With them all in the same room for the first time in years, there's no telling what drama will ensue... The only thing for certain? Fraser's inheritance bombshell will turn the billionaire brothers' entire lives upside down. And as for their love lives? Well...they'll be turned inside out too!

Find out in this fabulous new miniseries:

Cinderella's Billionaire Boss by Michelle Douglas

City Girl in the Outback by Ally Blake

Stuck with Her Impossible Ex by Kandy Shepherd

The Billion-Dollar Heir Returns by Rachael Stewart

Dear Reader,

I'm such a lover of cities—the skylines, the hustle and bustle, the well-cut suits. I tend to write about people who love the same, meaning I don't often have the chance to pen stories set in the vast, disparate wilds of Australia.

So, when this chance came along, bringing with it the wonderful writers joining me in unearthing the secrets and tragedies and rich family connections of Kings Reach, a noted (made-up) cattle station in Australia's rugged far north, I bit deep.

Sending my city girl, Mackenzie, into that environment, and watching her fall in love with the place, was an absolute kick. As was writing a hero rugged enough, strong enough, capable enough to live up to such a place. Still waters run so very deep with my glorious Fitz, and watching Mack—with her curiosity, vivacity and her refusal to back down from a challenge—disarm him so thoroughly made me absolutely giddy at times.

I hope their love story, set against one of the most beautiful, greatly untouched places in the world, gives you all the romantical joys as well.

Love,
Ally

Ally Blake writes warm, wistful, whimsical romance love stories, with over four million copies savored by readers around the world so far. An ardent advocate for romance literature, Ally delights in sharing her enthusiasm on air, in print and onstage at festivals across Australia. When she's not dreaming up happily-ever-afters, you'll find her sipping strong coffee, cloud-gazing or relishing in the glide of a dark pencil over really good notepaper. Winner of a 2024 Romantic Book of the Year award, Ally lives and writes in the leafy western suburbs of Brisbane. Find her at allyblake.com and @allyblakebooks.

Books by Ally Blake

Harlequin Romance

Billion-Dollar Bachelors

Whirlwind Fling to Baby Bombshell
Fake Engagement with the Billionaire
Cinderella Assistant to Boss's Bride

One Year to Wed

Secretly Married to a Prince

Italians of Vermillion

Dating Deal with the Italian
Fake Dating the Italian Heir

Crazy About Her Impossible Boss
Brooding Rebel to Baby Daddy
Dream Vacation, Surprise Baby
The Millionaire's Melbourne Proposal
The Wedding Favor
Always the Bridesmaid

Visit the Author Profile page
at Harlequin.com for more titles.

For the unrelenting fact-checkers, the intrepid investigators and the rigorous tellers of truths. And for my gorgeous Veronica, who cried when I told her the bones of this story—may your darling heart forever be so warm.

PROLOGUE

Last day of Autumn, Kings Reach,
Western Australia

FITZ KING RAN a finger beneath the bow-tie pressed to his throat as he eased his way through the glittering crowd filling his family's big converted barn, while calculating when he might slip away from the ball into the cool, late autumn night.

Small talk was not Fitz's thing—big talk neither, for that matter. The fact that he lived on his family's cattle station in the heart of the Kimberley meant that usually wasn't a problem. With the sheer number of guests who had descended upon Kings Reach in the hopes some King success might brush off on them, that evening he'd had his fill.

Breathing in as he slipped between two groups distracted enough not to notice him, he couldn't catch even a whiff of the hay bales, spare bridles and saddles, and busted machinery that had filled the dusty corners of the barn a week before. Now gargantuan potted palms in golden pots stood sentry by the doorways, ivy and fairy lights wrapped around the criss-cross of support beams above, and dozens of dainty cocktail tables covered in bark-brown linens filled the space, each with a centrepiece stacked with sprigs of Sturt's desert pea, fluffy tufts of mulla mulla, and shrubby Grevillea, as if they were fancy roses rather than scrub blossoms.

Fitz might have thought it was all a bit much, if not for the fact it was a celebration of his mother, and the many charities she'd championed during her life via the Eliza King Foundation, on the tenth anniversary of her passing.

When a federal MP caught Fitz's eye, he let his gaze slide past and kept on walking. He'd have been perfectly happy talking shop with any of the locals—"local" being those who worked the millions of hectares of ruggedly challenging crop and cattle-grazing country in the north-west of Australia, or the visiting Elders from Gija Country with whom the King family enjoyed a long working relationship. But the ring-ins, their private planes and helicopters currently resting wing to tail in the Kings Reach airfield, could find someone else to talk at.

At least Hideaway Haven, the ecotourism adventure and experience business Fitz owned and ran on Kings Reach land, was booked solid for the next few weeks by those who'd decided to make a holiday of the opportunity. Not that there was ever a problem booking out, but the low turnover of guests would give his staff a breath.

When the band started up again, playing a jazzed-up Bowie classic, head down, Fitz eyed the nearest side door, only for his next step to falter when he spied a woman by the far wall, chin down, moves almost comically stealthy as she skirted the crowd in a near mirror to his own approach.

There were too many people milling between them to get a proper look, but he knew she was a stranger all the same. Half the people in the place were unknown to him, but he'd have remembered if he'd met *her*.

It wasn't only the way her slippery-looking dark blue dress shimmered over her body when she moved, or the paleness of her skin that made him wonder if she'd ever seen sunlight, that had him pulling up short. It was the fact that she was so clearly on a mission and was not to be deterred.

When she paused, like a roo hearing the crack of a stick underfoot, then ducked behind a potted palm, Fitz coughed out a laugh of surprise.

Fingers appeared within the frond of the palm, then a pair of eyes filled the gap, only for a leaf to slip her grip and flick her in the mouth. Stepping out from her hidey-hole, the woman's tongue swept over a pair of glossy red lips, checking all was well. Then, hands on hips, she looked to the sky for help.

Now this *is entertainment*, thought Fitz, a grin tugging at the edges of his mouth.

"Fitz King has made the right move," accounted a familiar voice to his left, and Fitz glanced in that direction.

When he looked back towards the potted palm, the woman was gone. *Dammit*, he thought, with more enthusiasm than he'd felt all night.

"Diversification is the future."

Fitz recognised the voice as coming from a cattleman, not much younger than he, who'd likely driven the several hours from his station to be there.

"Poppycock," scoffed a bandy-legged gent older than Fitz's own father. "Cattle's the way. Waste of time and energy putting resources behind anything else. Fraser King, at least, ought to know better."

Several heads nodded, agreeing that breeding beef, moving it, and selling it was everything in these parts. And that Fraser, Fitz's father, was indulging his youngest son.

If only they knew Fitz had been leading a nice life before his mother had fallen ill—surfing the world's most glorious beaches, climbing the most unforgiving rock faces, leaping into the wild blue yonder, feeling life flow through every molecule in his body at every turn.

If only they knew how much his larger-than-life father had diminished, needing him, needing any one of his sons to come home, after Eliza had died.

If only they knew that his father's agreement to lease Fitz the land on which Hideaway Haven ran was the only reason he'd agreed to come home for good.

But they would never know, for the Kings were as famous for closing ranks on private family business as they were for their unsurpassed generational success on the land. Which was why the conversation, thankfully, moved back to cattle.

Wait... There she was again.

The stranger had done a U-turn and was closer now. With her back to him, he could see that her dark hair was like a waterfall of mahogany silk, and when she looked sideways, the back of her dress fell in a low dip, revealing the most touchable looking moonlight fair skin.

Someone stopped her. A man, offering a hand in introduction. Fitz saw her shoulder rise, then with a determined shake of her head, she spun on her heel and walked in the other direction.

What the hell? he thought, following her at pace, utterly transfixed. But that was soon overtaken by a more pressing question: *Who* is *she?*

He knew many of the locals—having attended School of the Air at the same time with a few, such as Charlie Ashwell, who worked on the Reach on occasion and was playing drink waitress that night. Or from bachelor and spinster bush dances he'd crashed with his older brothers. He'd even dated a fair few when he'd first got his driver's license, earning himself a reputation as a heartbreaker. When he'd finally cottoned on that the expectation for farm girls was to get married, have kids, and find future security in the merging of farming families, he'd never dated locally again.

The longest relationships he'd had since had been with Hideaway Haven and his horse. He just wasn't a forever guy.

The stranger hesitated and turned, her face in three-quarter profile as something, or someone, across the barn caught her eye.

Fitz dared not check who that might be, lest she disappear on him again. There was also the fact that he was close enough now to note her mouth was a curious pout, as she nibbled at the inside of her lower lip. Her eyes lively, bright and full of mischief. He could all but feel her energy crackling under his skin. For the stranger was not only lovely, he was now certain she was up to no good.

Jewel thief? Industrial spy? Hitwoman? Only thing he was certain of was that he did not care.

When frown lines puckered over her nose as she looked around nervously, Fitz held his breath. Then, grabbing a bowl of chocolates wrapped in silver paper from a nearby cocktail table, she tipped every last one into her purse and snapped the thing shut, before slipping into the crowd and disappearing once more.

Fitz lifted his hands in frustration and looked about him to see if anyone else was getting a load of this. The "anyone else" he had in mind were his brothers, all of whom were at the ball that night.

It was a strange feeling, thinking of them in such a moment. As, while the King brothers had been tight growing up, this was the first time they had been under the same roof in over a decade. Not even their mother's funeral had brought them all home in time.

Logan was easiest to spot as he was the tallest person in the room. Older than Fitz by a couple of years but older in the head by centuries, he was the King family lawyer. He lived on the other side of the country, in Sydney, and as Fitz saw it, found plenty of reasons to keep it that way.

Tom—second oldest—was currently chatting up Charlie and her drinks tray. The self-professed comedian of the family, Tom was the Kings Reach financial advisor. He also lived in Sydney with his daughter, Bea. Fitz had a soft spot a mile wide for the kid, and so as far as he saw it, Tom needed no excuse to do whatever she needed.

Then there was Jackson—the oldest of the King brothers. A builder of international hotels and the empire that came with them, Jack had made it clear over the years that he wanted nothing to do with Kings Reach. On one infamous occasion he'd told a journalist that he'd happily burn the place to the ground. Yet, somehow their father had lured him here for the ball, for there he stood, twenty feet away, chatting with a pair of Federal parliamentarians as if it was totally cool and normal.

While it should be a good thing, having them all there, for Fitz it meant there had been no avoiding the fact that there was one King brother who was not, and never would be again.

What would Will have thought of a night like this? His twin had been gone since they were both nine years old, so Fitz could only imagine a watery version of himself, which was just so unfair.

Turning to leave, when the need for fresh air suddenly became necessary, Fitz spun, only to run smack into someone. Apology ready on his lips, he reached to catch them as they teetered, only to find himself looking into the face of *The Stranger.*

You, he thought, as a pair of dazzling hazel eyes blinked up at him.

She knows who I am, Fitz realised, when her eyes widened and she sucked in a breath on a quick gasp. And the need to know who she was, what she was up to, drowned out every other thought.

When her top teeth clamped down on her bottom lip, and she seemed to melt a little in his hold, again he thought, *You*, only this time it was an amorphous thought, bringing with it the strongest urge to let his hands slide down her arms, reach around her back, and find that soft bare skin as he drew her slowly closer.

When the vision threatened to run away with itself, Fitz figured an introduction was the more gentlemanly way to go. He opened his mouth to ask the stranger's name, when someone called his.

"Fii-iitz! Yoo-hoo! Fitzy!"

Fitz looked to the caller to find a local farmer's wife, her daughter trailing apologetically in her wake.

And he felt the stranger gently untwist herself from his light embrace.

No, no, no, he thought, turning back in time to catch her giving him one last heart-stopping look, the kind that made men go into battle, conquer kingdoms, carve faces onto the bows of ships, before she spun away and melted into the crowd.

When Fitz's phone buzzed in the inner pocket of his tuxedo jacket, he was so not in his own skin he actually flinched. Yanking the thing free, he saw Tom had sent a message on the rarely used brothers' group chat. For the first time in years his brother was sending out an SOS.

Fitz strode through the crowd till he found Tom and Logan out the side door of the barn, where light from inside spilled out onto the back lawn, before it was swallowed by the winter's eve night.

"What's up?" Fitz asked, by which he meant, "It had better be good to have dragged me away from her."

"Jack's on the move," said Logan, as he strode off into the darkness.

Fitz swore and looked to Tom, who gave him a tight-lipped smile.

For all that he'd not expected a teary reunion when he'd heard Jack was coming home, he had assumed they'd find time at some point to share a beer, or a hug. A chat about their father. Future plans. But the truth of it was, despite all that bound them—memories both halcyon and needlessly tragic—they no longer knew how to be around one another.

Then Tom loped after Logan, and Fitz jogged to catch up.

While for Logan "serious" was a default setting, Tom leaped at Fitz and attempted to put him in a headlock. Fitz, younger, quicker, grabbed Tom's hand and twisted it behind his back in a way that had Tom crying uncle even as his laughter brushed up against the silence of the night.

Rubbing blood flow back into his arm, Tom added, "You been working out?"

Fitz, who'd never seen the inside of a gym in his life, punched Tom lightly in the shoulder. Tom shot Fitz a warm grin that had so much of Bea in it, Fitz decided the next headlock would be a freebie.

"Stop messing about, you two," Logan grumbled over his shoulder.

Tom mimicked Logan perfectly, and Fitz chuffed out a laugh. Then the two of them caught up to Logan, jostling him till he jostled back as they followed Jack into the Never Never.

As Logan and Tom gravitated to walking side by side, Fitz hung back, taking in the cool night air, the hum of cicadas in the tufty grass, the occasional leathery flap of bat wings swooping low overhead.

And allowed his thoughts to slip back to the willowy brunette.

If only he'd had another five minutes, what would he have done? Followed her about the room, just to see what she'd get up to next? Casually asked if she had any snacks in her bag? Asked her to dance? Invited her to spend the night in his bed?

Logan kicked something, swore, then, muttering under his breath, turned on the light on his phone.

City boy, Fitz thought, jogging ahead to stay clear of the light pollution. His instincts had always been in tune with the land, which is how he knew where Jack was leading them before one of the others murmured, "The waterhole."

They slowed as they arrived at the spot, while Jackson, lit by stars and moonlight, came to a stop beneath a tree by the bank. Not just any tree—the tree in which Jack, one summer, had built Will's tree-house.

When Jack reached out and curled his hand around a branch, Fitz's heart heaved against his ribs, and a slew of memories came flooding back. Will using the tree-house to birdwatch, sketch, avoid their father's constant disappointment. Logan up there, planning out one of his intricate scavenger hunts. Tom and Jack, leaning against the tree, talking about girls. Fitz, the daredevil even back then, spinning wildly on the tyre, his older brothers yelling, certain this time it would snap.

Now there was nothing left, bar the rope missing its tyre.

"So, Jack," said Tom, and it was a miracle he'd held his tongue that long. "How's tricks? All good with you the last...several years?"

Logan shook his head at Tom's approach, but still moved to back him up.

When Fitz, not a huge fan of confrontation, veered away from the scene, Tom noticed and took the temperature down a notch. "Wish I'd had a heads up we were meeting like this. I'd have taken a moment to snag a bottle of champagne and some glasses."

"What are we toasting?" Logan asked.

Mum, Fitz thought with a twist in his gut, knowing she'd have been destroyed seeing how uncomfortable they all were around one another. Her love for her boys had been ferocious, and she'd raised them to be one another's greatest defenders.

"To Mum," said Tom. "Miss you to bits." Then, "And to Will. Wish you were here, bud."

Fitz swallowed, throat biting as if he'd downed a bottle of bubbles.

Then Tom added, mirroring Fitz earlier thoughts, "I wonder what Will would have made of all this, of us right now?"

"Are you interested in knowing what I make of you all now?"

Fitz spun on the spot to find their father standing on the slight rise leading down to the waterhole.

Claiming the high ground, Fraser King looked every inch the patriarch of a generationally successful cattle station in his custom tuxedo, greying hair swept rakishly off his deeply tanned face, silver sprinkles in his thick brows and short beard.

In the silence that followed, he stared his sons

down, one by one, before his gaze landed on Jack. Something obscure flashed behind his eyes before he said, “Why am I not surprised to find you all down here?”

What did that mean? That he had been hoping to find only one of them? Only *Jack*?

Then Fraser notched his shoulders back, cleared his throat and said, “Well, it's serendipitous, as I've something to say that concerns you all. Something I've been thinking about for some time, and I've come to a decision. I've hired lawyers—”

Logan took a half step towards their old man. “Lawyers? I'm the station's lawyer.”

“Not in this instance. You've a vested interest.” A muscle worked in their father's cheek, then something seemed to click into place behind his eyes. “I've started proceedings to break the irrevocable trust.”

Fitz's mouth dropped open. Literally. The irrevocable trust had been set up after their mother had passed from kidney disease that came on fast and taken her quickly. It had been her final wish—the backbone of which meant that not only would Jack, Tom, Logan, and Fitz inherit Kings Reach and its associated holdings in equal measure, they would have equal say over its future.

Despite tensions existing between the brothers even then, Will's death having messed with them all in different ways, their father had honoured her wish without even a hint of hesitation. In the years since, its preservation had never been in doubt.

Logan paced. Tom had bent over, hands on his thighs, Bea no doubt top of his mind. While Fitz, every muscle coiled tight as a cornered snake, glanced to Jack just as Jack looked to him. But at that distance, Jack's response was inscrutable.

Was *this* the motivation behind the floral arrangements, the fact the minister of primary industries would be sleeping on their back lawn, the big band playing Mum's favourite songs? Was it nothing but a ruse to bring them all here…for this?

But then Fitz remembered how his mother and father used to slow dance in the kitchen to Little River Band. Remembered the whispered conversations they would have as they headed upstairs together every night. Remembered how humbled his giant of a father had been by her loss.

Logan asked, "What's the alternative? What do you plan to do in its stead?"

Fraser's jaw worked as he looked each of them in the eye. "When the time comes, management of Kings Reach will fall entirely to one of you." A beat slunk by before he said, "To Jackson."

Fitz flinched. For his father might as well have lifted a hand and slapped him across the face. Not that he'd have asked for such a burden at the expense of his brothers, but had the last several years he'd spent back on Kings Reach meant nothing?

"Why?" Fitz asked, his voice as brittle as sunburned glass.

Fraser barely glanced his way, yet in that half second Fitz saw years of alienation, disappointment, back-breaking work, and compromise backing up in the man's gaze. Enough that Fitz was braced for it when the axe finally fell.

"This is what your mother would've wanted."

Done with this, Fitz turned on his heel and headed back up the rise.

Tom called out, telling him to come back, but Fitz kept walking. He'd seen how obstinate his father could get when times were hard, when the weather was vicious, when staff did not pull their weight. He'd seen how tough he'd been on Will.

But *this is what your mother would've wanted* was brutal.

It was the exact opposite of her hopes for them all, certain to stir up ancient gripes and guilt that Fitz had hoped time, and space, and maybe even this weekend might have demurred.

Then Jack's cool, cultured voice wafted after him. "Do you care about your legacy so little you'd leave it to the one man who'd see it divided up and sold off to the highest bidder?"

Fraser's voice came next, thin compared with Jack, and aged, despite the stridency of his words. "When you get down to it, it's just real estate. And real estate is your superpower, Jack."

Tom called, "Fitz, come back."

Fitz ripped the bow-tie from his neck and shoved it in his pocket, then called out, "I'm going back to the party while there still is one. I have to see a girl about a dance."

Only, while the thought of finding the willowy

brunette and losing himself in her flared brightly for a heady moment, Fitz did not go back to the party.

Instead, he walked. And walked. And walked. All the while kicking himself for thinking that by coming home, by being the example to his brothers, trying to find some kind of peace with his dad, he might be able to find a way back to the way things had been in the before.

He should have known better. He'd lost enough in his life to know there was no coming back.

While the urge to walk away as he had done once before—no responsibility, nothing keeping him tethered—was overpowering, he'd connected himself to this place by way of Hideaway Haven. He had staff counting on him. And he was proud of the thing, *dammit*.

He'd stay on the Reach. But no more, no more needing anything or anyone. Allowing himself to love something the way that he had this land was just asking for heartache.

Lesson learned for the last time.

CHAPTER ONE

Four months later...

IT WAS A month into springtime Down Under when the luxury four-wheel drive carrying Mackenzie Lawler across miles of barren red dirt, through dry flood plains, and over rivers trickling with brown water, pulled to a scrunching halt outside what could only be described as the palatial homestead at the Kings Reach cattle station.

The fact that she was already thinking in terms such as "Down Under," rather than the more correct "north-west region of Western Australia," irritated the back of her tongue like a sour sweet.

For while Mack wished to be pounding London pavements, gathering anonymous sources, uncovering injustices, instead she had been sent to the other side of the world to pen a peppy puff piece on Hideaway Haven, a high-end ecotourism business that, from the research she'd done thus far, was doing just fine without her.

While her driver took care of her luggage, Mack squinted through the tinted windows, taking in the grey-green scrub, the fine ochre dust covering anything not on the move. She was definitely not in London anymore.

"Well," she told herself, "a great reporter writes great reports, no matter the circumstance." And she wanted nothing more than to be a great reporter, so she was going to write the best damn feature *The Pulse* news site had ever seen.

Shoulders notched, Mack swished the car door open only to be smacked with a kind of heat she had never experienced. The light so bright it seemed to shimmer around her, and yes, that was sweat collecting in unmentionable places.

She did not remember it being anywhere near that hot the first time she'd stepped foot on Kings Reach land. Then again, the day of the Eliza King Foundation Ball it had been near winter, and she'd been jet-lagged, famished, and high on the fact she'd flown halfway across the world on the kind of journalistic hunch they made movies about, while also mildly panicked that someone would figure out she'd crashed their party.

"Miss?"

Mack smiled at the driver and followed him to where he'd stowed her luggage under a shaded wooden pergola, where, upon a hand-carved table beneath a large mesh cloche sat a plethora of fresh fruits, crackers and cheese, crystal cut glasses, and a sparkling jug of iced water with slices of lemon floating dreamily atop.

Nice touch, she noted, tucking the imagery away

for her piece, while also hoping lemon slices would not be the highlight.

Luxury wilderness travel, exclusive nature-based retreats, Mack mused, quoting the Hideaway Haven website as she turned a slow circle to find gum trees, tufts of dry grass, and old wooden fences that appeared to have been patched many times over.

Not that she'd taken a proper "holiday" to compare it with in a truly long time. She worked. All the time. If having no time to date, or take holidays, or live any kind of normal life is what it took to land her dream career, writing for a *real* newspaper, then so be it.

Only after her escapade, her editor's boss—the director of news and content for the Lawler Media Group, who also happened to be her much older half-brother, the venerated Crispin Lawler—had made it clear she was lucky to still have a berth at *The Pulse*, much less anywhere else. And the only way for it to stay that way was to stop "colouring outside the lines," stop "getting in her own damned way," and writing the pieces she had been assigned.

"Head into the shade, miss, before you burn to a crisp," the driver said, his Australian accent broad. "We must be a smidge early, or someone from Hideaway Haven would have met us. Stay put. I'll let them know you're here."

"Thank you," said Mack.

"I'd say have a great stay, but folks call it life-changing." With that, the man loped off towards a pretty two-storey cottage to the side of the main homestead, the roof shaded by a gargantuan tree with a widespread canopy and lush red flowers.

Life-changing, Mack echoed. What she'd give for that to be true.

Giving her first impression a second chance, she took in the burr of crickets, the soft whisper of hot breeze through dry leaves, the nearby whinny of a horse that matched the scent of livestock on the air. Then something huge and fuzzy buzzed in front of her face, and with a squeak and a madly flapping hand, she swished it away.

Mack's phone buzzed several times in the pocket of her cream linen dress. Delighted to find a strong signal after miles of patchiness, she hastily scrolled through the texts from Priya, her favourite editorial assistant and fact-checker extraordinaire, who had been helping her with background research for the article.

Which, for Priya, now meant sharing many *many* pictures of the King brothers, Mack realised, as she scrolled past a picture of Tom King in what looked like a pickup game of basketball. Logan King behind a lectern guest lecturing on law at the University of Sydney. Jackson King on a work site, looking over engineering plans.

That last one made Mack's tummy turn.

The entire premise behind her hare-brained hurtle across the globe four months earlier had been to corner Jackson King, question him regarding rumours he was attempting to circumnavigate heritage laws stopping him from tearing down a much-loved old hotel in the West End, and come home with an exclusive that would shake the very foundations of London city planning. Sexy stuff.

At the very least she'd hoped it would catapult her from the playful, buzzy, culture-lite *The Pulse*, where she'd been working for several years now, and onto a permanent desk at *The Indicator*, the revered, century-old masthead that had made the Lawler family keystones of the British media establishment.

Alas, all she'd come home with was her tail between her legs.

Mack scrolled down to Priya's final text, eyes widening as a photo of the youngest of the King brothers filled her screen.

There was Fitz riding a wave, hair flicking wetly across his face, the top half of his black wetsuit hanging at his waist, impressive six-pack on display. Then there was Fitz hanging from a rock face by his fingernails, profile all tense concentration, tight climbing gear leaving little to the imagination. And lastly, Fitz, tanned creases fanning from the edges of his dark blue eyes as he squinted into the distance, ski goggles holding back long hair with sun-brightened tips, his face all hard angles, and rough stubble, an honest to goodness work of art.

Mack typed her response.

MACK: Not quite the citations on Western Australian sustainability standards and conservation I was expecting.

PRIYA: If I send any more "background" there'll be no room for new stuff. Or fun.

MACK: I'm not here for "fun."

PRIYA: What if it finds you?

PRIYA: Last thing. Reckon he still has that V disappearing into his jeans area? Must research to uncover correct term.

Mack, flushed, turned her phone over and laid it on the table and tried her best not to think of Fitz King's Adonis belt. Yes, she knew the term. For while she was apparently too "excessively work-focused" and "exceedingly ambitious" to "be in a relationship"—all direct quotes from when she used to have time to date—she wasn't a nun.

Of all the King brothers she might actually run into at some point during her stay, it had to be *him*. Not nice-looking Tom, or earnest-looking Logan. Not even austere Jackson. But Fitz—the very reason her plan to corner Jackson and befuddle him into giving her a career-changing story had unravelled previously.

Once she'd made it inside the ball, after hours spent practicing exactly what she would say, waiting for the right moment to pounce, she'd seen her moment, only to have a run-in with Fitz King.

A collision, more like. Dazed, she'd looked up and up and up, and… Well. Fitz King was a striking man—big, broad, with thick wind-swept hair. That was saying nothing of the banked heat in those smoky steel-blue eyes. Or the size of his hands, holding her upper arms as if he'd feared she might swoon. Which, to be fair, had been a possibility.

By the time she'd remembered she'd been on her way to dazzle Jackson, the eldest King brother was gone. Neither that night, nor the next morning before the guests all rolled out, had she seen any member of the King family again.

All this was running through her mind when the scratch of boots against dirt had Mack looking up to find a man loping towards her—long legs encased in blue jeans, blue button-down shirt over a broad chest, riding boots kicking up dust. A cowboy hat sat low over his face, casting a shadow that left only his mouth and stubbled jaw spare, but by the frisson of awareness scooting through her, Mack knew exactly who it was.

When Fitz King slowed, Mack stood, heart rate quickening. Only partly due to the mighty testosterone wave coming at her, mostly because she hoped he'd not remember *her* at all.

If, by some miracle, he did, she'd explain herself, of course. But if it did *not* come up, then she would really love to let the whole embarrassment die a natural death. There had been no harm done, after all.

The man slid his hat from his head, ran a hand through thick damp hair, then his loping strides slowed to a stop, as his gaze landed on her several pieces of matching luggage.

Some definite thoughts were being thought before his gaze lifted and his eyes met hers. And all she could do was stand there, while something hot and scratchy skittered through her.

"You heading out to Hideaway Haven?" he asked, by way of hello.

Mack blinked at the rough depth of the man's voice. "Ah, yes. My driver went to find someone. Might that have been you?"

Fitz, frowning, looked over his shoulder. When no one else appeared, he turned slowly back to her and said, "Welcome to Hideaway Haven, Ms…"

"Lawler," said Mack, her name like a snap on the warm wind compared with his drawn-out drawl. Then, "Mackenzie Lawler. From *The Pulse*."

And…nothing. Not a flicker of recognition at her name, or the name of the website. Or her face, for that matter. And while she'd just been telling herself that would very much be for the best, it was a little deflating to say the least.

Needing to get back on track, Mack took a forthright step out into the sunshine, where she hissed as she lifted an arm to cover her eyes, the brightness of the sun threatening to sear away the top seven layers of her eyeballs.

Fitz King's quick-as-lightning smile at her expense, while troubling, was a thing of dreams. "You okay there?" he asked.

Mack, holding herself together most ably, sent him a deadpan, "I'm certain your website never said anything about packing surface-of-the-sun-level protective gear."

"I'll let our IT department know," Fitz drawled, tipping his hat back onto his head, his voice turning velvety soft, with a slight scrape at the end that felt like sandpaper against her insides. "Mackenzie, did you say?"

"Mack's fine," she offered, stepping towards him and holding out her hand.

A beat went by before he said, "Fitz King." Then his hand slid against hers.

His skin was brown against her pale fingers, calloused and a little rough, and she felt a spark snap right in the centre of her palm.

"Well, I am thrilled to be here," said Mack, taking back her hand and curling it in on itself in the hopes of stopping the tingle that remained. "I'm so looking forward to writing your story."

"My story?" he repeated.

"The story of Hideaway Haven. For our super popular Weekend Edition. Our audience will be utterly obsessed by the time I'm done with you."

The man's gaze, now seriously dark and stormy, bored into hers. "Where did you say you were from?"

"*The Pulse.* British news website. I believe my

editor, Alicia, has been liaising with your guest experience manager." *What was his name again?* "Ned! You run an exceptionally popular venture, Mr. King, as it's taken us a couple of months to be able book a long enough stay for me to…to really find out what's going on around here."

At which point he looked hard into her eyes, and Mack's heart fluttered like a trapped bird against her ribs. Had he finally recognised her?

"You're a *reporter.*"

Mack balked. "A… Well, yes." So, no, he hadn't recognised her. If she kept this up it was going to be a long stay.

Needing for this assignment to go well—no flying monkeys or blunders of any kind—Mack brought out her most conciliatory smile. "Mr. King… Fitz. I can assure you I'm not here to unearth any skeletons in your closet. I am here to experience what you have to offer, then to spread the word to a ravenous audience with disposable income, hungry for fresh, Instagram-able experiences."

Fitz took off his hat and once again ran frustrated fingers through his thick chestnut hair, only this time a fold of hair curled broodily against his forehead, like some kind of teen-love-triangle heartthrob. Not that she watched those kinds of shows as a twenty-eight-year-old woman. Okay, she did, religiously, but only because in her position one had to be *au fait* on the zeitgeist. And it was the only place she got her romance fix these days because she was so busy chasing stories, writing stories, or wishing she was chasing or writing stories.

Mack bit her bottom lip, understanding a little then why her editor had thought some time out in the naughty corner might do her some good.

"Look, Ms..." said Fitz, jabbing his hat back on his head with such finality it snapped her back to the now.

"Lawler. Mack," she repeated, smiling through clenched teeth.

"We have grown to what we are via word of mouth among a community of people who value our mission. We attract clientele who take what we do here seriously. I have no interest in being Instagram-able. Or anybody's obsession."

Mack swallowed, not because of the way his gaze had most definitely dropped to her mouth on his final word, but because her job was hanging in the balance.

While she'd love to be on her way back to actual civilisation, if she went home with nothing to report, she might never have the chance to report something for the Lawler press again.

And yet, it seemed Fitz King was not yet done.

"We can't have Haven or Reach staff handholding some city reporter for the next however long. The Haven is fully booked with a high turnover of disparate guests. As for the station, the wet will be on us soon enough, meaning full station musters, weaning calves, branding, tagging, sorting stock, moving them to higher ground."

Mack's instincts, which had felt tremulous for months, perked up, brushed themselves off, and cocked an ear. Yes, everything the man had said had merit, but surely the guy was protesting too much.

Question: If so, why?

While she was absolutely, definitely not going to even think about writing any story bar the one she'd been expressly sent there to do, allowing her investigative muscles to stretch after cowering in a dark cave for so long couldn't be a bad thing.

Needing to lock this thing down, Mack reached into her bag, pulled out a notebook and pencil, and play-acted preparing to take notes.

Fitz blinked at her. "What are you doing?"

Mack blinked back. "This is gold dust. For my article. Glamping among the rugged and rough reality of the far north while big burly blokes in blue button-downs ride the range? It practically writes itself."

Snark was risky, but it so often paid off when coming up against a huffing, puffing alpha male. It showed she wasn't there to faff around. The glint of respect she saw flash behind the man's eyes told her Fitz King was no different.

Then, frowning as if it was his favourite thing, he said, "Then here are the rules."

"Rules?"

"Ways and means of not getting eaten in the night."

Hearing a rustle in the bush nearby, Mack bit the inside of her bottom lip and nodded.

"First rule—listen. If I, or any Haven or station staff, offer instruction, it is not a suggestion or a fun little anecdote. Things can turn on a dime out here, so what we say goes."

Mack's grip on her pencil tightened.

"You'll be supplied with a backpack. It has a GPS locator built in. Never leave your accommodation without it. Not for a stroll, or a meal, or even for a bush wee. It means we can keep track of where you are at any time."

"*Any* time?"

"You are smack bang in the middle of millions of hectares of some of the least forgiving terrain on the planet. We're talking sudden gorges, plunging escarpments, treacherous tidal flats, sparse desert, crocodile-infested waterways. That's not taking into account flash flooding, regular forty-plus degree days, and the fact our nearest neighbour is a five-hour drive away. We are remote, we are hazardous, and when it comes to those under our care, we do not take chances."

Well, Mack thought. The sudden dryness in her throat far less to do with the scare Fitz King was trying to stir in her, than watching the man morph into Captain Australia, right before her eyes.

As if he knew *exactly* what she was thinking,

his eyes darkened, then he drawled, "Write that in your little notebook."

Mack knew an insult caged in artlessness when she heard it. Yes, her notebook was small, but the ideas within it were mighty.

"Is that it?" she asked, voice cooler than she felt.

"For now."

"Excellent. Now here are *my* rules. And before you protest, just as your profession has certain requirements in order to run as safely and efficiently as possible, so does mine. Fair?"

Fitz crossed his arms in such a way the fabric of his shirt strained against his biceps, and her insides needed a moment to realign themselves.

"An interview a day," she said. "You and me." It was excessive, but the hot-tempered little voice in the back of her head wanted to see the man pale.

"Not possible," he shot back, unfazed. "Aside from the Haven, this is a working cattle station. Any time I am required to look after guests or livestock takes priority."

"Fine. Then let's agree to…ten hours, minimum, over the course of my stay."

Fitz's jaw clenched before he nodded.

"You can read the piece, but only when it has been submitted, and only for fact-checking purposes. You have no editorial say."

She feared, with the next-level jaw clenching going on, the man might break a tooth.

"I will talk to whomever I please on the property," Mack went on, "so long as it does not interfere with the running of the station or your business. I will ask whatever questions I please, and you and your staff have every right to answer, or not, as you see fit. There will be no judgement or assumptions made by me either way."

Fitz looked dubious, and it put to mind how infamously Jackson King refused to talk to the press, ever.

Questions: Was protecting their privacy a family trait? Or was there a reason for his reticence?

Not the story, she reminded herself.

"That said, if anything is to be considered off the record, the speaker must let me know *before* information is shared. And it must be explicit. So you know, 'off the record' does not give you legal protection, but in this case is an agreement between parties. And my word of honour."

Fitz breathed out long and slow. "Are you an honourable person, Mack Lawler?"

Mack remembered the last time she'd found her way to this place, and the lengths she'd gone to get there. But while her method may have been chaotic, her motivations, she was determined, were pure.

"I like to think so," she said, chin up, holding his steely gaze. "How about I take you at your word that you won't drop me off a cliff the first chance you get, if you take me at mine."

Her words hovered between them, like a dare. And the longer she looked into those mesmerizing eyes, the warmer her cheeks became, till she felt as if she was falling under some kind of spell.

Then a warm breeze came out of nowhere, rustling her skirt and flicking at her hair, and something shifted in Fitz's gaze. For a second, she even thought she heard music, like an echo of the band playing at the ball when this man had held her in his strong hands.

Then the "music" became voices, and over Fitz's shoulder Mack saw her driver exit the cottage, and behind him came a humongous young man in much the same get-up as Fitz.

"Oh, hiya," said the younger man in a strong Irish accent after they'd waved the driver off. "Aren't you the lucky one. Not often we see the big boss out here, welcoming the guests. Hope he did you right, miss?"

Fitz gave the guy a side-eye that had him lowering his head in mock subservience. Then he said, "Ms. Lawler, this is Caleb, one of our wilderness guides. Caleb, this is Mackenzie Lawler—"

"Mack," Mack interjected, reaching for the Caleb's hand and smiling when she was smiled at. When they shook hands there was no zap at all.

"She is a *journalist*," Fitz said, his voice deep with warning. "I'll be answering any questions she might have beyond what any guest would usually ask of you. Understand?"

"Aye, aye, sir," said Caleb with a salute and a breezy grin.

To Mack, Fitz said, "Caleb will take you through the initiation."

Caleb held up a tablet.

"More rules!" Mack clapped her hands with glee.

"Many rules," Caleb agreed cheerfully. "Number one of which is that Hideaway Haven resides on a working cattle station and so, for the safety of the livestock, and our guests, some areas are out of bounds."

He handed her an A4 laminated map with waterways and topography both easy enough to identify, Hideaway Haven outposts, and the Kings Reach homestead and working lands.

"Stick to the green," Caleb said, pointing out the swirls of red, orange, and green. Then he held out a tan leather backpack. "Satellite phone, first aid kit, another larger, more detailed waterproof map, water skin, shelter, GPS tracker—lots of goodies."

"Chic," she said, nodding in excessive appreciation in Fitz's direction. Was that a puff of laughter? If so, he hid it behind a cough, before glaring at the world as if it had done him dirty.

"You're staying at The Ridge the first half o' your stay?" Caleb asked after pulling Mack's details up on the tablet.

"If you say so."

"We have a winger on our hands. The Ridge is our series of eco-cabins—built on the edge of Garnet Gorge. The views are truly something to write home about."

Feeling Fitz's hard gaze on her still, Mack only half paid attention to Caleb's talk of how to face down a drop bear as she brought out her "little notebook," turned the page with an exaggerated swish, pretended to lick the end of her pencil, and with a look of fierce concentration on her face, scribbled madly.

Out of the corner of her eye she saw Fitz turn and walk away, and something inside of her slumped in relief, as if she'd spent the past fifteen minutes teetering on the edge of some precipice and was finally on solid ground.

And while it was not exactly in her purview, she wrote:

> Question: If Fitz did not want me here, how is it that I've ended up here at all?

CHAPTER TWO

LEAVING CALEB TO his charm offensive, Fitz strode away from the Hideaway Haven drop-off point, determined not to look back.

It had been four months, and yet the moment those bright, overcurious eyes had fixed on him, he knew. It was *her*—the willowy brunette in the slinky blue dress, the chocolate thief, the stranger from the ball.

He'd been on the verge of saying something—*where did you go, sorry I never came back, you were a highlight on a rough night*—only his tongue had tied itself in knots. Thank the gods, for she'd not given any indication that she remembered him at all.

Now that some distance had quieted the heavy pulse beating behind his ears, he realised she'd also not mentioned that she'd been to the Reach before at all.

That was strange. Right?

Hell, maybe it was nothing. He was on edge about everything these days. Firstly, with his father in bed "with a cold" all week long, meaning he'd had to juggle Reach and Haven business more than usual. And secondly, with either Tom or Logan calling him on a daily basis with updates on their plans to stop their father from breaking the irrevocable trust. Jackson, at least, had fled the country shortly after their father's announcement, and despite the brothers' group chat being on fire since that night, he'd at least left Fitz alone.

When Fitz reached the cottage, he slowed and took out his phone. He knew *The Pulse*. It was innocuous enough. The family behind it was not.

The Lawlers were to the British media and communications what the Kings were to cattle. Their papers had unearthed corruption, brought down governments, unravelled more than one monarchy. Now one of them was staying, right when his family was in the midst of the most tangled upheaval since… Well, since losing Will.

His thumb hovered over the chat icon, then he saw the chat name. It had changed multiple times over the years, mostly at Tom's doing. Full of Bull, Royal Pains in the Grass, The Throne Room—now it was Fence Sitters Anonymous. A very clear dig at Jack, and himself.

He knew Tom and Logan were frustrated by his perceived lack of action in trying to change their father's mind, but unlike Tom and Logan, who were good with their words, Fitz had always been more of a doer.

He'd come home, and he'd stayed.

The first time he'd left had been after his parents had thrown him a blowout eighteenth birthday party; a bunch of his first-year uni and School of the Air friends had come to stay, and it was a wild weekend. Then right in the middle of a rowdy game of beer pong, it had hit him—he was entering adulthood and his twin never could.

He'd packed a bag and left home the next day, finishing his business degree on the road, and making it his mission to pack his life so full it was enough for two lives.

Remembering how Tom had ribbed him, calling it his Danger World Tour, while Logan had regularly asked if his travel insurance was up to date, Fitz slid the phone into the back pocket of his jeans, ran his shoes over the mat by the door, took off his hat, and went inside.

The air conditioning hit like he'd walked into a freezer. And Ranger, the Haven's resident long-haired kelpie, lay in a soft bed covered in blankets in the corner. His chin remained leaning on his crossed front paws, but his tail thumped against the floor at the sound of Fitz's footsteps.

"I just met Mackenzie Lawler," Fitz called when no one looked up. "In case you were hoping she'd slip by me unnoticed."

Julian, standing at the main desk, lifted a finger as he finished typing with his other hand. "Hmm?"

"A journalist," Fitz said. "From London. Her editor has apparently been liaising with Ned for some time."

Julian looked to his partner, Ned, who was dutifully dripping water onto the succulents little Bea had gifted—aka forced upon them—when last she was there.

Julian and Ned were the guest experience managers at Hideaway Haven. Experienced climbers and adventure junkies when he'd first met them, they'd been lured away by Fitz from their day jobs in finance in Manhattan with the promise of the great outdoors, and they'd never looked back.

When Fitz threw his arms out in frustration, Ned sighed. "Told you he'd have a fit." Then, "The direction came down from on high."

On high? What did that even—

"Do you mean *Fraser*?" Fitz asked, incredulity lifting his voice a good octave.

First the wild notion to break the trust, then the plan to leave the running of the place to Jackson, the one King least interested in a King family legacy, and now *this*? His father had nothing to do with the Haven; he barely acknowledged its existence. So why would he enter into such an agreement?

None of it made a lick of sense.

"Look," said Julian, holding up both hands in surrender. "After your father insisted it was happening, we vetted her. Great numbers, nifty little writer, a favourite at *The Pulse* despite her nepo baby status. But if you need me to send her home, just say the word."

Fitz pictured the woman, all twinkly-eyed, with that notebook and pencil poised as if he was about to tell her the meaning of life. Yeah, Mack Lawler was most definitely going to be trouble.

And yet… "She's here now. Sending her away could only hurt us."

"Great!" said Julian. "The staff have already been apprised. They know to treat her as they would any other guest, and if they are asked any questions beyond the scope of her Haven experience, to refer her to us. We can add you to that list."

"Amend that," Fitz said. "I am the list."

Julian dutifully made a note. "And who did we choose as her guide?"

The Hideaway Haven wilderness guides were mostly a mix of locals who, not keen to work their own family cattle stations, barramundi farms, or sandalwood plantations, had come to Hideaway Haven to drive or guide groups, or lead hikes and canoeing tours and the like. Caleb was one of a slew of backpackers who had made their way to the Reach and stayed.

"Caleb," said Ned. "Most likely to show her a good time, and I swear that boy could wrestle a croc and come out on top."

Ned was right, and yet a wave of discomfort shot through Fitz. "What other new groups are coming in this week?"

Julian wiggled the mouse, squinted at the computer screen, then listed off the guests, where they were staying, what experiences they had signed up for.

Before he could talk himself out of it, Fitz

told them to move Caleb to a group coming the next day. Knowing he should take on the role, he couldn't, not with his father out sick.

"Is Sinclair free? Put her on the reporter." A super-experienced Adelaide-based hiker and registered nurse, Sinclair was smart, dry, loyal. And not Caleb. "Tell her she'll be escorting the reporter to The Ridge in fifteen minutes. And tell her I'm coming with them."

One foot out the door, Fitz turned back. "Ned, when you're next fiddling with the website, add a disclaimer. May need to pack surface-of-the-sun-level protective gear."

Ned blinked.

Then, feeling slightly better about things, Fitz stepped back out into the Kimberley sun.

Twenty minutes later, Mack sat in back of a huge bruiser of a Land Rover, not nearly as flash as the one that had driven her there from Kununurra, rocking side to side as they drove up a dirt track leading away from the Kings Reach homestead.

The drive in had been impressive, but now that she was in the thick of it, the scope of the Kings Reach property was staggering. They'd passed horse yards and stables, working barns as well as the one used the night of the ball, which now appeared to be empty, and so many outer dwellings she couldn't imagine how they might all be used. Then, suddenly, there was nothing but Outback as far as the eye could see.

Sinclair, who had arrived from nowhere to take over from the charming Caleb, turned to look over her shoulder from the front passenger seat. "How are you going back there?"

"Fine and dandy," said Mack with a smile.

Meanwhile Fitz, deft fingers maneuvering the car over the rutted road, big shoulders hulked against the leather seat, the mis-fold of his collar against the chestnut brown hair curling over his neck, quietly ignored her.

So Mack asked Sinclair, "How did you end up working for Hideaway Haven?"

Sinclair opened her mouth, but then Fitz cleared his throat.

"Not long now," Sinclair said with an apologetic smile. "The Ridge is only about five kilometres from the homestead, an hour's brisk walk. While The Rise is the more 'Outback' experience, The Ridge is my favourite of the two spots. Bit more upmarket and fancy, you know?"

Mack did not know, but she would soon enough. At which point she would have to come up with her *own* series of suitable scintillating superlatives that would make *The Pulse* salivate over the chance to visit.

Mack's gaze lifted to the rearview mirror to find a pair of steel-grey eyes locked on to hers. All smoky glints, and tanned creases, and dark criss-cross lashes.

The urge to poke out her tongue was so strong, she instead gave the man a beatific smile, then went back to looking out the window, hoping it wouldn't be too much longer, or with all the juddering she might well lose her lunch.

"We've won the West Australian Kimberley Ecotourism Award the last three years running, and the national award the last two," said Sinclair as she heaved Mack's luggage out of the back of the Land Rover.

"Impressive," said Mack, as she took in what was to be her home for the next while.

The eco-cabin was, as Sinclair declared, an impressive structure. A white A-line corrugated roof boasted an array of solar panels on one side, and a small chimney on the other, leading to the assumption that it wasn't always hot enough to make a girl's crevices "glisten," as her mother used to say. At the bottom of the canted roof, windows ran along the entirety of the sides of the structure, while the looming two-storey-high façade was all gorgeous smoky glass.

Thump. Thump. Thump.

Mack turned to find Sinclair yanking her largest suitcase up the dozen wooden steps leading up to the accommodation.

"Allow me," said Mack, but then a tan leather backpack appeared right in front of her face. Rearing back, she turned to see it was hooked on Fitz's pointer finger.

"Cheers," she said, lifting the thing free and placing a strap over one shoulder.

"Our love and knowledge of flora," Sinclair called out from right behind Mack, as she grabbed the remaining bags, before jogging back up the steps, "fauna, history and country, alongside our consistent sustainability ethos, is the heart of the Hideaway Haven experience."

Quietly, just for Fitz, Mack asked, "Anything you'd like to add that I can't find on your website?"

A muscle at the edge of his mouth flickered. "It's a pretty thorough website." Then he glanced pointedly in the boot as if checking just how much more luggage she'd brought with her.

Rolling her eyes, Mack and her backpack took the stairs to join Sinclair on the triangular patio at the front of the structure. And when Mack took a breath to ask a question, Sinclair swept a hand in an arc and said, "Look."

Mack turned, looked, and thought, *Oh my.*

If the architecture of the cabin was impressive, the view was something else. Small hills rolled away to the left and the right, all rich vibrant red dirt pocked with rocks and scrub and spots of bright flowers. And straight ahead, beneath the deep purplish-blue of the great dome of a sky, the land seemed to just…drop away. As if a giant had clawed out the gorge beyond with its bare hand.

A delighted laugh escaped her lips as her gaze dropped back to the car below. Or, to be more specific, the man leaning against it, arms crossed, ankles too, dark eyes watching her beneath the shade of his hat.

“Look!” she mouthed, pointing, and the man dipped his chin, just enough all she could see was the curve of his smile, before he pushed himself away from the car and went for a stroll.

“Come check the place out,” Sinclair called out, and Mack followed her inside.

“Kitchenette,” Sinclair said, pointing out each amenity. “Mini fridge, solar powered with backup battery. The satellite Wi-Fi can be sporadic, but the weather looks good the next few days so you ought to be fine. Food will be delivered daily. Till then, you’re stocked up with organic, locally-sourced fresh fruit, muesli, yoghurt, breads, condiments, dinner options, snacky snacks, water, wine and beer. Around back, there is a composting toilet and enclosed shower in case you don’t want the audience that comes with the outdoor tub.”

“The audience?” Mack asked, deliberately not imagining the man wandering about down below.

“The wallabies can be a curious crew,” Sinclair said with a laugh.

“Any other visitors I ought to be concerned about? Creepy crawlies and the like?”

“There are spiders, of course.”

Of course.

“Redbacks are the real nasties. Mostly find those under your outdoor furniture, so check before you sit. Huntsman—the ones that are around the size of a kid’s hand—are harmless. They mostly appear when it’s been dry for a while as they come inside in search of water.”

"Right," Mack croaked, her mouth having gone dry. "Good to know."

"Then there's the slitherers," Sinclair went on, moving out onto the patio and leaning her hands against the railing as she squinted at one tuft of grass then another. "Some of the most dangerous snakes in the world are found in these parts. The western brown—fast and aggressive buggers. Then there's the mulga, and the death adder."

Mack made a mental note to ask Priya to send her a thorough list.

"Goannas are the big fellas." Sinclair held her hands as far apart as possible. "You'll often see them halfway up a tree. Freshwater crocs can go after you when threatened, but it's the saltwater you really need to stay clear of. You don't plan to set off on any solo hikes?"

When Mack said nothing, Sinclair looked down the hill to where Fitz had meandered back to the car and called out, "Solo hikes?"

After a long beat, as if allowing himself a moment to imagine Mack being mauled by some local creature or another, Fitz shook his head.

Mack doubted she'd even leave the cabin at this rate.

"It's all in the welcome pack," said Sinclair, "which you'll find on the lamp table by the chair. Caleb told you about the map. Green is good. And..." Sinclair picked up the backpack Mack had left on the patio and held it out for her.

"I have to wear this thing *everywhere* I go?" she asked, putting the thing on.

"Everywhere you go," said Sinclair, her expression earnest. "It's for your own safety."

Suddenly this felt less like an assignment, and more like a hazing ritual.

Only Mack wasn't entirely sure who was hazing her.

Alicia, her editor at *The Pulse*, had been the one to organise the trip, to get her out from underfoot. It was possible Crispin didn't even know she was here at all.

Being a Lawler was one thing. Being a Lawler who had only found out she was a Lawler after her mother died, her birth certificate revealing her to be the illegitimate daughter of Sir Maximillian Lawler, leading to her father's wife, Deanna, taking her in after finding out she had nowhere else to go, was a whole other barrel of snakes.

She was certain that Crispin, who had long since moved out of Lawler House before she came on the scene, kept her on in the family business, not because he saw her potential, or appreciated her moxie, but because it was the only way he knew how to show a sense of familial duty.

Sinclair clapped her hands enthusiastically, snapping Mack from her fugue.

"Anything else before we leave you to your first night?" Sinclair asked as Mack and her backpack followed her down the steps to where the car, and its broody driver, awaited.

When no one spoke, Sinclair glanced from Fitz, to Mack, to Fitz, and they both shook their heads.

"Okey-doke," Sinclair said. "As your official wilderness guide, I've left my phone number with the info pack. Call or message anytime. Till then, welcome to Hideaway Haven!"

Sinclair jogged around the side of the car and hopped into the passenger seat, leaving Mack and Fitz to stare one another down in the sudden silence.

After a long beat, Mack crossed her arms to mirror his stance, but it took her adding a scowl and pursing her lips for Fitz to shift in place.

"Have you ever worn a backpack in your entire life?" he asked.

She turned to show him. "I think it suits me. I might even take up walking after this."

"Hiking?"

"Walking. Till now I've been rather partial to a driver."

Fitz smiled, a flash of a thing that was over before it began. But, *oh my*, was that a dimple in the man's right cheek? Mack might never recover.

Then something in the bush nearby made a noise and she nearly jumped out of her skin. "I'll head up now."

"You'll be right," said Fitz.

Inexplicably, by his intonation, Mack knew it wasn't a question. And despite the instant antagonism that had sprung up between them, the fact that he seemed certain of her ability to spend a night on her own out there felt akin to beatification.

"If I'm not devoured by a spider the size of a dinner plate, what time should we meet up tomorrow to start the interview process?"

The man looked at her as if she'd asked when it might be convenient for her to pluck out his leg hairs one by one.

"Ten a.m. work for you?" she nudged.

"Sinclair is your guide. She'll organise any experiences you wish to try."

Having seen this coming from a mile away, Mack said, "Excellent. I can't wait to hang with Sinclair some more. I get the feeling she's a chatty sort. Readers of *The Pulse* do love a gaff, so I can't wait to find out about times things have gone awry—"

"Tomorrow," Fitz said through gritted teeth.

Then, lifting a hand to his hat, he tipped it in a quick goodbye, before sliding into the driver's seat of the Land Rover. With a wave out the window, and a kick of red dust beneath the wheels, the car trundled back in the direction from whence they'd come.

Remembering the litany of slithery bitey things out there, Mack hurried up the stairs, closed the screen door and the glass behind it, and checked the lock, twice.

Then she grabbed her phone, took a photo

through the window and sent it to Priya, then climbed up onto the gorgeous king-size bed, opened her laptop, and began to type.

CHAPTER THREE

HER FIRST NIGHT at Hideaway Haven, Mack slept rather well. She woke with a glorious stretch, opening her eyes to gentle sunlight dappling the floorboards of her cabin.

After trying the outdoor shower and scoffing down homemade muesli with creamy locally produced milk, she went to call Fitz only to realise that in all the hubbub she'd forgotten to ask for his number.

Halfway into Sinclair's guided four-wheel-drive tour of Garnet Gorge, while holding on to her hard hat as they traversed a meandering cave system boasting stunning curtains of limestone stalactites, she asked, "Do you know what time I should expect Fitz?"

"For…?"

"Our interview."

Sinclair's silence under the crunch of boots on the gravel floor did not bode well. Then, "I'm fairly sure he's on tail-end calf marking and branding prep for the overflow today, as Mr. King has been under the weather this week. But I can check what time they're due back this evening?"

Mack swallowed down her disappointment. "Can you ask him to call me when he gets back?"

Sinclair assured her she would, then explained how up ahead they'd see rock formed into what looked like frozen waterfalls, all the while Mack's story radar was going *zing, zing, zing.*

Questions: Fraser King, infamous cattleman, patriarch of Australia's greatest cattle station, was *unwell*? How unwell? Was that a regular thing, or was this unusual? What on earth did "tail-end calf marking and branding prep for the overflow" mean?

That was not her story, she reminded herself.

Even so, she jotted the questions in her "little notebook," all of which would later go into her online Future Stories file for Priya to collate and pretty up.

She'd once read her father did much the same thing in the spirit of collaboration with his fellow truth finders. While his version had been scraps of paper, notes written on coasters, kept in a shoebox under his desk, Mack had an open-source file she or any one of her fellow *The Pulse* reporters could refer to if needing something for a story one day.

When they returned to The Ridge after lunch, she took the afternoon to finesse the questions she'd ask when she did get the chance to interview Fitz.

Only to go to bed not hearing a word.

* * *

On her second morning at Hideaway Haven, Mack woke with a start to a cacophony of screeches and squawks outside her cabin. Then there had been the constant *click, click, click* that had sounded late the night before. Certain it was coming from inside, she'd sat at the head of her bed, torch grasped in her hand, googling "what noise do spiders make?" until she had eventually fallen into an exhausted slumber.

Yes, her place back home had its idiosyncrasies with its temperamental plumbing and tiny staircases—but she'd never appreciated the triple-glazed windows more.

By the time Sinclair picked her up, promising a fun surprise, Mack was more than ready to talk to Fitz, but instead found herself on a light plane tour with a nice man named Ray, who took her on a low-level scenic flight to Lake Argyle, over the Bungle Bungles and home again.

And while it, again, was stunning, with Ray pointing out the curve of the Pentecost River, the bright auburn cliffs of the Cockburn Ranges, a dust plume from a four-wheel-drive vehicle on the outskirts of an abutting station, she only listened with half an ear, realising that not only had her employer sent her to a place she would not get underfoot, it seemed Fitz King had done the same.

Dust motes glittered in bands of sunlight slanting through gaps in the timber of the stable walls, bouncing off coiled ropes hanging over long rusty nails and halters with leather cracked from years of sun. Add the scent of sunbaked straw and damp earth, linseed used to oil the saddles, and the musky undertone of animal sweat, and to Fitz the stables felt like home.

It was also a nice place to escape to when the resident humans were doing his head in.

Yesterday his father had flown to Broome without letting anyone know why, then that morning he was out on the station as if nothing had happened. And there was still the fact he'd unilaterally brought a reporter to the station without consultation.

Then there was Sinclair, telling Fitz she was afraid Mackenzie Lawler might stowaway on the roof-rack the next time she drove up to the The Ridge if she didn't get to talk to Fitz soon.

"Okay, girl," he murmured gently, when his stock horse, Yini, blew a raspberry, clearly telling him to get on with the cool down. Then he lifted the hose to run water over her flank and brushed her down, cleaning away the sweat and dust after that morning's ride.

When Fitz's phone buzzed in his pocket, then buzzed again, he tipped the hose into the water trough, wiped his hand on the relatively clean front of his shirt, and checked to find several messages from Tom.

TOM: We're coming down for the weekend. Can you make time?

TOM: Bea misses her Uncle Fitz to pieces. And her granddad, can you believe.

TOM: And she wants to make sure everyone's watering her succulents.

Fitz huffed out a laugh at Bea's list of must-sees. But his smile was short-lived at the thought of Tom, and Bea, and no doubt Charlie, Tom's fiancée, landing there, full of fizz and chatter with Mack Lawler just down the way.

Fitz went to tap out a *how about a couple of weeks' time*, till he wondered if this was really the best moment to tell Tom there was a journalist staying at the Haven, or if it would only add fuel to the fire.

Remembering Mack Lawler where he'd left her standing on the bottom step leading up to the cabin, looking at him with that intense, far too clever gaze, the wind catching at her hair, sunlight turning her pale skin to soft gold, he grabbed the hose, held his phone away from him, and ran the cool water over his head.

Only when Yini snickered, huffing out a warm breath, hooves stomping, tail flicking, then Ranger, who had been sunning himself outside the barn doors, let out a series of soft woofs, did Fitz look over his shoulder to find Mackenzie Lawler standing in the doorway of the stable.

For a second he thought he'd imagined her there in that floaty white dress, the sun shining through it making it near translucent, the outline of white underwear curving low at her hips. But even before she lifted her hand in a wave, he knew she was real, as for the life of him he'd never have dreamed up *floral* cowboy boots.

Fitz glanced around for Sinclair; but no, they were alone. Meaning…had she *walked* the entire way? Going by the tendrils of hair stuck to her neck, and the way she was flapping her dress, sections sticking to her thighs, it seemed to be so.

Fitz pocketed his phone, turned off the hose, and walked towards her, blood whumping in his ears as he imagined all that could have gone wrong. Heat stroke, snake bite, trip and fall—it was not fair country out there, especially for those not suited to its extremes, which this wayward city girl was so clearly not.

He stopped a good two metres away, whistled for Ranger to come to heel, and growled, "What in the ever-loving hell are you doing here?"

Grruubbblsjuufuubbb, thought Mack. Or something of that ilk.

Her brain felt like mush, partly because she had lost half her body weight in sweat on the walk from The Ridge to Kings Reach. But by that point it had felt like her only option, otherwise Fitz King would find a way to stymie her story every day till she left.

Following the map—"green bits only" be damned—had been easy enough. Despite her "I am partial to a driver" quip, she'd been known to enjoy a walk on occasion—Harvey Nicks, Sloane Street, lots of great places were doable in under an hour from home on a nice day when the tube was down. Though the dress—which, back home, was a favourite breezy option on a hot day—turned out to be a seriously wrong turn.

The rest of the mush brain was all down to walking in on Fitz King standing in a beam of sunlight, shirt unbuttoned, jeans riding low on his hips, hosing himself down.

"Don't blame Sinclair," she said as he glared at her.

"Why would I?" he asked, his voice dangerously low. "When I have you standing there looking like guilt incarnate."

She held up a hand in front of her face and said, "Your shirt."

"What about it?" He looked down, grabbed the edges of his wet shirt, flapped it once, twice, revealing flashes of dark hair under his arms, his Adonis belt on full show.

"It's hard to concentrate when you look like… that."

The man slowly buttoned a *single* button, and said, "You've yet to answer my question, Ms. Lawler. What are you doing here when it was made clear to you on day one that this place is out of bounds?"

"Would that be the same day you agreed to be interviewed? Because if you are constantly sticking to the non-green zones, it puts us at rather an impasse."

Their gazes held for an interminably long time. Then Fitz surprised the heck out of her by murmuring, "Touché."

Taking it as a win, Mack moved into the shade of the stables, only for Fitz to step to the side, as if allowing her even a fraction closer might break some other rule she wasn't privy to. Several horses poked their heads over stall gates, but unlike the dressage stables Deanna had taken her to when she'd first moved into Lawler House, there were no neat navy velvet riding helmets or shiny knee-high black boots to be seen.

She looked back to Fitz, to find his gaze on her. Or, to be precise, the trickle of sweat slithering slowly over the dip at her collarbone before disappearing beneath the fabric now stuck to her damp chest.

When she swallowed, Fitz blinked, frowned, then dragged his gaze to his wrist, where a heavy-duty watch, the kind that could survive a hurricane, nudged up against what looked to be a frayed, pink-and-orange friendship band.

"As luck would have it," he said, "I have a small window of time right now."

"You do?" she said, tone only slightly dripping with sarcasm. "Well, isn't that lucky."

She looked about for a pair of hay bales, or some place they might sit for a bit, till Fitz sighed.

"Come on," he grumbled. "Follow me."

Fingers trailing over shelves filled with an impressive array of colourful paperbacks and vinyl records in the downstairs library at the Kings Reach homestead, Mack remained quietly shocked that Fitz had let her within fifty metres of his family's home, much less inside.

With its blond wood floor, acoustic guitar resting against a side table, large rattan baskets filled with throw blankets slouched against beautiful mismatched leather sofas and chairs, it was the kind of room one might find in the architecture and design pages of *The Indicator*. It was also charming and esoteric, and offered a glimpse into a wealthy Outback family she'd not have expected.

Not that that was her story.

The slap of bare feet on wooden floor had her turning towards the door to the house as Fitz rejoined her, after taking a minute to "dry off." And when she gazed past him to the Federation-style panelled walls and terrazzo tile beyond, Fitz's large form stepped in front of her view, and he closed the door with a pointed snick.

"Red zone," he said, pointing a hand at the door. "You do not step past that spot, ask questions about that spot, or even think about life beyond that spot."

"Got it. That was a lovely horse you were brushing down."

Fitz paused at her quick change of topic, and she could see him trying to decipher if her comment was a trick. Which, of course, it was. The time had come to put aside the fun and games and make the man feel comfortable enough to talk.

"Where had you come in from?" she asked. "Sinclair mentioned you were doing something with calves and overflow the other day. Unless overflow is a personal subject. To you."

So, a little fun and games might still be required every now and then, just to get the conversation flowing.

Fitz rolled a shoulder as he moved away from the door. "This morning, we were checking fences along the nearest southern border of the property. A dozen cattle marked with the Kings Reach brand had been called in roaming free near Durack Crossing."

"All fixed?"

"All fixed."

"Cows found?"

"Cows found." A beat, then, "Though the proper term is cattle."

"Ah." She knew that, of course. Letting him feel as if he was teaching her something would ready him for when the real questions began. "Sit. Get comfy."

While he did so, Mack wandered by the small table covered in family photos. At the very back was the one photo of all five of the King brothers, including Fitz's twin, Will, who she knew from her research had died young. One twin was grabbing one of the older boys in a headlock, the other was tucked up under Jackson's protective arm. She wondered which was which.

"Tell me about this room," she said.

Fitz, who had taken a seat in a red leather wingback closest to the recently closed door, said, "Home. Out of bounds."

"You were very clear that everything on *that* side of the door was not up for grabs. Meaning this room, and everything within it, is."

He could enforce the same rule by simply refusing to speak on it, but she was testing how far she could push.

And it worked. "This was my mother's favourite room in the house."

Eliza King, she thought, *in whose honour the ball in the barn had been held.*

Mack paused, wondering it that might be the perfect moment to say, *Oh, by the way, I was at the ball. And, now that I think of it, didn't we almost meet there?*

Only the memory of the moment—how it had felt to be up against him, those steel-blue eyes gazing deeply into hers with such intense clarity—had her courage skittering into a hidey-hole.

"What did she love about it?" Mack asked, picking up a small carved bird, then putting it back down.

Fitz slowly leaned forward, feet flat to the floor, elbows on his knees. Looking to the bookshelves, he said, "She was a big reader. For whatever reason she made it her mission to make sure I was too."

Mack offered an encouraging smile and a big gaping load of silence, and Fitz, clearly not used to being interviewed, filled it.

"She constantly had multiple books on the go. Upstairs books, downstairs book. She loved a great dramatic romance, but read any genre. Any era. Being from the city, originally, I think it helped her feel connected to the outside world."

Mack tried to imagine how it might have felt for Eliza to come to this vast, hazardous, isolated fiefdom, leaving all conveniences, friendships, family behind, and found she could not come up with a reason powerful enough that she could imagine *ever* making such a choice.

"And the albums?" she asked.

"We've all added to the collection over the years."

Mack slipped one free to find *The Best of Englebert Humperdink*. Showing it to Fitz, she asked, "Yours? Your brother's? Your dad's?"

A knowing smile lifted the corners of his mouth as he shook his head—boundary reached.

"Okay!" she said, spinning till she found where she'd dumped her backpack. "If you're happy for me to do so, I'll record the interviews. It will mean any quotes will be verbatim, which protects you as much as it will help me."

After a few beats he nodded.

Taking a seat across from his, she pressed Record, then said, "This is Mackenzie Lawler speaking with Fitz King in the library at the Kings Reach cattle station, on a beautiful spring day in October in the Kimberley, Western Australia."

She set the phone on the coffee table between them, then looked him in the eye and said, "Fitz, tell me the story of how Hideaway Haven came about."

CHAPTER FOUR

FITZ HAD BEEN frustratingly reading the same page of a Dick Francis book for an hour, his mind caught in a loop, wondering if he'd been bamboozled by a bumptious journalist the day before, or if the interview had actually gone okay, when Ranger's nose bumped his elbow, asking to be let out.

Marking the page using a bookmark Bea had made, Fitz let the dog out the front door of the Hideaway Haven cottage for his morning constitutional.

A water run with Perry, the station manager, on the cards that morning, he looked to the distant sky. The dawn sun was just starting to colour, and while there was some cloud to the east it was not enough to worry, yet enough to keep an eye on.

Knowing there was little point heading back to his book, he stepped off the front porch and made his way around the shrubbery separating the cottage from the homestead. Living above the Hideaway Haven offices was far better for his mental health than knocking around inside his childhood home with his father, but there was no getting around the fact that the coffee machine at the big house was far superior.

He made his way around back, towards the library, the door there never locked, only to think of the interview again. Talking about himself was always excruciating. Doing so while up close and personal with Mack, her gaze bright with interest, had been torture. But not because of her questions—he'd been close enough to count the smattering of tiny freckles scattered across the bridge of her nose. To wonder if her walk from The Ridge had brought them out, or if she'd been using the outdoor tub that came with her cabin? If so, where else had the sun left its mark?

Fitz ran a hand over his face as he stepped up onto the wraparound porch of his family home, Ranger's claws clicking behind him.

Instant attraction was not new to him, but this felt different. From the moment he'd first seen her at the ball all those months ago he'd felt as if he'd been lassoed by some invisible rope. The ball she had still not admitted to attending, despite the fact he'd broken his own rule and brought up his mother.

Fitz was so deep in thought, he didn't see Annalise, his father's PA, sitting on the bench outside the door till he was upon her.

"Morning," Fitz said.

Annalise flinched with such vehemence she nearly fell off the bench.

When she made to stand, Fitz held out a hand.

"Stay. I was heading inside to make a quick coffee. Want one?"

"No thanks," said Annalise, settling back on the bench as if glad to be off her feet, which for a little before five in the morning was a nod to how hard she worked. Not only had she knocked the Reach's unruly admin into shape with her bright, busy, no-nonsense way, she'd organised every last tablecloth, flower arrangement, and travel plan for his mother's ball.

In fact… "Anna, would you know the invitation list for my mother's ball off the top of your head?"

"Gosh, no. But I can get it for you if you need it."

When she *again* went to stand, Fitz stayed her with a soft laugh. "It's not important."

Nodding, she reached for a cup of tea sitting on the ground at her feet by a dozen terracotta pots, each boasting a small cactus she and Bea had spent some time "planting" when Tom and Charlie had been in need of some "private time" when last they'd visited.

Remembering Tom's message the day before, Fitz made a mental note to get back to him.

Annalise sighed after taking a sip of her tea.

"That good?" Fitz asked, as he shucked off his shoes.

"Heaven in a cup," Annalise said with a half-smile. "I finally convinced your father to import some in, when he caught me near crying over the kind Mrs. McRae had brought in on the last shop drop."

"Atta girl," Fitz said, before hauling the library door open. "Now, I'd better get in and out before Mrs. McRae finds me, or she'll want to feed me, or wash my clothes, or cut my hair."

"Or marry you off to one of her grandkids?" Annalise asked.

"You too?"

Annalise held out her hand for a low five, which Fitz gave as he stepped inside.

Only to see her unwrapping a small chocolate from silver wrapping before popping it into her mouth.

"Is that… Is that the chocolate from the ball?"

"Mmm-hmm." She leaned forward and, glancing past him to make sure the way was clear, she whispered, "We still have a couple of boxes left. I had to hide them as your father kept finding them."

Fitz huffed out a laugh, then glanced inside. "He up?"

"For some time. He and Perry have already taken the ATVs on a water run."

Fitz's blood ran cool as Anna's words sunk in.

Perry, whom they'd hired a few years back when Fraser had busted his knee, had made plans with Fitz to help out on that job. Now his father was up and at 'em, it seemed Fitz was surplus to requirements.

One day he was in favour at the Reach, the next he was out. One week leaned on by the management team who were well aware of his knowledge and skills, then the next slung back into redundancy. It had been a perpetual tug of war since his return, and if that was his own fault for not going all in, he could never be sure.

Misunderstanding his hesitancy, Anna gave him a small smile. “Go. While the house is all yours.”

“Right. Ta,” he said, only to turn back one last time. “Which is the good tea?”

“Yorkshire Gold. Gold packet. Hidden behind the other stuff.”

Fitz knocked on the door-frame in thanks and headed into the house.

Mack made her way through yoghurt and berries, and three pieces of toast, as she waited for Crispin to join her video call. It had only taken around a half-dozen messages to his assistant to make it happen, and it was after midnight in London before her brother found a minute to spare.

Half-brother, she reminded herself in the hopes of making it smart a little less. While she’d spent the sixteen years she’d known she was a Lawler trying to form a relationship with him, it felt as if he’d given her a job and thought, *There, that’ll do.*

If Mack was anything she was tenacious. And while taking every class his mother, Deanna, had offered in the hopes of finding common ground, and working her tush off to attend the same university he had, hadn’t cracked that nut, she *knew* that writing something that blew his damn socks off would. It had to. For after that she was all out of ideas.

Then, there he was—glasses perched on the end of his nose, vest and tie over a crisp pale blue shirt, a purposeful, dapper forty-four to her twenty-eight, and the youngest Lawler ever to be in charge of the news division. An honour that had come at a cost, when their father—a man she'd *not* managed to ever form a relationship with, good or otherwise—had died of a heart attack several years earlier.

"How's the piece coming?" Crispin asked with zero urgency in his voice.

"Great!" she said. "The Kimberley is a phenomenally beautiful and interesting spot. There are a *hundred more* stories I could tell about this place. The relationships between indigenous groups and current land 'owners,' the state of the Australian beef industry. There's a local pilot, Ray, who has the funniest stories—"

Crispin's levelling gaze had her words dry up in her mouth. "Did Alicia ask you to gather a portfolio of pieces, or just one—the kind where you are unlikely to be arrested and we are unlikely to be sued?"

Mack swallowed. Would she *never* live that down? "I'm working on my assigned piece, I assure you. But if you get a chance, Priya, my editorial assistant, has access to my collaboration file, and she's a phenomenal collator, so if you find anything there you think has merit—"

"Surely Alicia can do that."

Alicia being her editor at *The Pulse*.

"Well, yes, but I'm thinking of a series of features for *The Indicator…*"

Ready for an instant "No," Mack's voice petered off.

When Crispin rubbed at the bridge of his nose and let out a long-suffering sigh before lifting his eyes to hers and saying, "We'll see," she nearly fell off her chair.

"Do the work, Mackenzie. Let me know when you're back, and we can have lunch."

Mack lifted her hand to say goodbye, but her brother was already gone. Likely onto the next call—some political dissident, or president of a multinational conglomerate, while she glamped in the middle of nowhere while the real world rolled on without her.

Then the sound of a car cut through the silence.

While she knew it was likely Sinclair, there to take her down a river, or up in a hot air balloon, or some other adventurous endeavour, her heart lifted into her throat at the thought it might be Fitz. Had she replayed her recording of his deep, measured drawl, while picturing him lounging in that beautiful library, all big and barefoot and sexy as hell? Several times over.

She moved to the glass cabin door, and when she saw the hardy old Land Rover, Fitz's car, idling in place, her heart gave a mighty *ther-dunk.*

Sliding the glass door open, she jogged down the stairs and knocked on the driver's side window.

Fitz jumped, as if he'd been deep in thought,

then took his time rolling down the window. The car still idling.

Mack said, "Well, hello, there!" rather more brightly than she might have had she had a moment to prepare.

Turning his hot, dark gaze her way, he looked her up and down. "What are you wearing?"

Mack glanced down at her denim overalls over a cute white tee with a tartan pocket. "It's farm gear."

"Says who?"

"Burberry."

When he still made no move to turn off the car, she leaned into the window, her forearms resting on the ledge. "What about you then?" she said. "With your blue jeans and your button-down shirts, sleeves always rolled up to the elbows, showing off your big strong arms."

At that a single eyebrow flickered.

"And your beaten-up cowboy hat," she went on, "ready to slide onto your head, so that you appear all cool and brooding the moment you step out of the car."

She'd been attempting to snag his attention, but instead he was now looking at her with a kind of intensity that was all rather heady when so up close and personal.

"Cool and broody?" he repeated, his voice dangerously low.

She attempted an insouciant shrug. "It's all a little clichéd, don't you think?"

At that Fitz turned slowly, till his elbow rested against the back of his seat, his face mere inches from hers. "Is this how you talk to all of your interview subjects, or should I consider myself special?"

"So says the business owner who welcomed a client by making it perfectly clear he did not want her to be there."

Fitz's eyes narrowed, even as his mouth kicked up at one corner.

Feeling the atmosphere shift and thicken, Mack's fingers curled around the edge of the window. Then she reached in, turned off his car engine, and took his keys.

"Coming in or what?" she called, before bounding up the steps to the cabin.

The first time Mack interviewed Fitz, he'd felt on the back foot. This time, blood still up after his fiasco of a morning, he was ready for her.

Sitting in a chair on the deck, he watched her flit about the cabin, putting together a tray of crackers and cheese and punnets of raspberries and bowls of walnuts. It was such a random collection of snacks, he assumed meal prepping for a hungry blue-collar man wasn't something she did often. Or ever.

Had she dated someone like him? Was she seeing anyone now? Not that it mattered—to him, or this process—it was simply a thought exercise while he waited: *What might it be like to date Mack Lawler?*

She wasn't the type to be a passive participant in anything, much less a romantic relationship. Or a single encounter. She never let the chance for an argument go by, meaning it would take someone willing and able to go toe-to-toe for it to have a hope of working.

Not that he was looking for something to "work." He'd made the decision long ago to never be in a position where he became so attached to another person that losing them would shatter him all over again. He had a great many skills, but putting himself back together in a whole and healthy way was not one of them.

And yet…

There was no hiding from the moments he'd spent over the past months imagining what it might have felt like to touch her hair, to run his nose down the side of her neck, to taste her—it lived inside him like a virus. Now, watching Mack lick flavours from her fingertips, humming if something appealed, he felt in her the same thing that had called to him at the ball—the need to keep moving, knowing, learning, that intensity of purpose.

Something he'd spent years trying to quash in himself, guilt eating at him that Will would never have the chance to do or be or feel again.

Fitz shifted. He'd thought of Will more over the past few days than he had in months. Was it having his brothers on his case? The fresh new frustration he was feeling towards his father? Or was it Mack?

There was a clever rhythm to her process, making it likely a person could bare their soul before they even saw it coming. But Fitz's soul was not for public consumption. It was a busted thing that no person in their right mind would want a bar of, and had been since he'd lost the kinder, softer, gentler half of himself. Whatever Mack thought she could get from him, she was only going to leave disappointed.

When she walked towards him, Fitz planted his feet on the ground.

"What kind of tree is that? The yellow one?" she asked, nudging her chin towards a bush covered in flowers.

Aware that she was getting him to look right while she figured out how to poke his left, Fitz said, "Yellow kapok. The flowers are edible."

Placing the tray on the table, she scooped up a handful of berries and moved to lean against the railing. One might think she'd been finding the shade; Fitz knew she'd taken the high ground.

Waiting for his permission to record, she then asked, "Do you believe ecotourism is only accessible to those who can best afford it?"

Okay then. If yesterday had been all ease and delight, this time she'd come to play. And Fitz felt that old hunger flicker to life.

His answer? "No."

"Just no?"

He nodded.

Her eyes narrowed, the metaphorical flapping

of a red cape at a bull. Then she said, "You were born into an extremely successful, generationally wealthy family, so the cost of living is likely not something you pay heed to. For example, a loaf of bread—"

Fitz shot off a number. When Mack's mouth popped open, Fitz cut her off again.

"That's the price of a loaf of bread at Kings Reach—retail, plus transport costs, by road then air. Now consider the hundreds of staff working on site, more seasonally, for the Haven and the Reach, and it adds up. So yes, the price of staying here for most people is high. But here you will feel as if you have stayed on the very edge of the earth, in a place filled with story and millions of years of history, the raw beauty and untouched majesty which will never leave you as long as you live."

Mack's chest rose and fell, her nostrils flaring, as if his return spar was as much of a thrill for her as it was for him.

But Fitz wasn't done. "We also have a program that ensures those who will benefit from being here, but do not have the means to, are able to experience it. We partner with the Lost Boys program run out of Darwin, offer scholarships for local indigenous students keen to earn agricultural degrees, and sponsor several low socio-economic secondary schools in the state, inviting their graduating cohorts the opportunity for practical skill gathering before hurtling off into adulthood."

When, instead of lobbing back her next question, a softness came over Mack's face, it snuck in behind Fitz's ribs and squeezed.

"How about you?" he asked, sitting back, voice gruff.

"I have no clue what a loaf of bread costs back home."

"I meant what is your mission? Why do you do what you do?"

"Oh." For a beat he thought she might refuse him, but with zero irony she said, "I want to write stories that matter."

"Why?"

She looked lost for a second, as if no one had ever asked that of her. "Because…they're the kinds of stories people remember."

"Do you want your stories to be remembered, or the fact that you wrote them?"

Mack coughed. "Wow. Look at you, going right for the jugular. Maybe you should be doing my job."

Fitz picked up his drink, the condensation dripping down the glass in direct contrast to the heat skittering over his skin, and, using her own trick, left silence for her to fill.

"Does it make me seem conceited to say the answer is probably both?"

"It makes you seem honest."

She blinked and coughed out a laugh. The flicker of cynicism at the end was a surprise. "Okay, honesty. My brother…half-brother, actually, runs the news division of the Lawler Group, while I write fizz and delight for their popcorn paper. So, there's that."

She looked out over the view for a second before adding, "But I also write to understand why people do the things they do—why they cheat, why they lie, why they love. How people choose who to care for, and who is below their notice. I want people to feel the consequences of their actions, but also find grace in the unburdening. For we all make mistakes, but we also need to be given the chance to do better."

As if she'd only just remembered he was there, Mack's eyes shifted to his. "Except *this* story, of course, which will focus entirely on the wonder that is Hideaway Haven and nothing more."

"Of course," he allowed.

The smile she gave him was self-deprecating, and it lit up her lovely face in a way that had Fitz struggling to find his next breath. He looked to his watch, noting the time ticking away, and Mack blinked and went back to her regular questions.

They talked about the differences between The Ridge and The Rise, the wilderness guides and their varied backgrounds and experience, the Haven's relationships with indigenous groups in the region. All easy, surface subjects, meaning he was distracted when she asked if his family had considered opening up his very large family home for more intimate homestays, so as to show people what life on a cattle station was really all about.

"Not happening," he said, the words landing with a thud between them.

While Mack's face remained impassive, there was the slightest flicker of her right eyebrow. On anyone else it might be a tic; on Mack *he* knew she'd caught the sniff of a story.

So, before she had a chance to get her hook in him, he reached into the bag at his feet and pulled out a handful of chocolates wrapped in shiny silver paper. Ambling over to where she stood, he unwrapped one, slowly, so as to let the paper crinkle damningly, and popped it into his mouth.

Leaning his backside against the railing by her, he asked, "Want one?"

She shook her head, her eyes a little overbright, he thought, as she stared at the collection in his hand.

"I never got to try one at the ball—my mother's memorial charity event, held here around four months back. They disappeared too quickly. Take some, even if only for later?"

Blinking furiously now, Mack plucked three chocolates from his still open palm and tipped them straight into the front bib of her overalls, then said, "I think that's enough for today."

Enjoying the fact that the high ground was now very much his, Fitz asked, "Do you ride?"

Her gaze flew back to his. "Ride?"

"Horses."

"Oh," she said, clearly flummoxed. "I… Yes. Of course."

"Excellent. I'll call the stables and let them know we're on our way. I've found myself in a rare patch of superfluity, so rather than keep Sinclair on the hook, you are now stuck with me. Lucky you."

"Lucky me," she said with a half-hearted attempt at a smile.

Yes, Fitz thought, scrunching the empty chocolate packet into a ball and tossing it into a bin on the corner of the deck, the high ground was a much more comfortable place indeed.

CHAPTER FIVE

When Mack said she could ride a horse she'd been telling the truth, only for her that had meant dressage lessons when she was thirteen or fourteen. She'd not been on horseback since.

While Fitz looked an absolute dream in his faded denim, hat low over his brow, button-down with the sleeves rolled up, showing off his big strong arms—gosh, had she really said that out loud—her teeth jarred as they trotted along the fence-line of a paddock, passing cattle slowly chewing on bales of hay. If she didn't get the hang of it soon, she might dislocate a hip.

Fitz glanced her way.

"Don't watch me," she said, tipping wildly when the horse shifted direction to avoid a large tuft of grass.

Ignoring her demand, he instead came alongside her and slowed their horses to a walk. "I have no choice but to watch you, Ms. Lawler, in case I need to scoop you up as you fall. Shall we turn back—"

Mack shook her head, determined to get the hang of the rock and the roll. "When I said I could ride I meant I had *ridden*, but then it was more a case of light walking around a freshly raked ring in a climate-controlled eventing hall."

"Fancy," he said, his voice a rumble.

She'd never met a man whose voice made her very bones shiver, but that's how it was every time he spoke. As if he put her under a spell. It was the only excuse she could find as to why she'd spoken of her relationship, or lack thereof, with Crispin. She must have sounded so ridiculously earnest. Not that he'd seemed to have minded.

She risked a glance his way to find his usually stern face was relaxed, his shoulders too. As if talking about himself took effort, but out here, on horseback, was his happy place.

"If you find that impressive," she said, when she realised she'd been staring at him for a good minute. "I also took piano lessons, fencing lessons, French and Mandarin. Silversmithing, oil painting, singing lessons, and…and that's it."

"That's it? That's impressive."

Mack smiled at his words. And Fitz actually smiled back. And a frisson of awareness shot through her.

Mack tore her eyes away and looked dead ahead.

Yes, the man was gorgeous. Yes, every time he shared some part of himself she was sure he didn't freely share with others, she felt as if she'd been given a gold star. But *smiling* at the man, *crushing* on the man, tingling in all kinds of fresh and exciting places anytime he glanced her way was not good. Or smart. Or conducive to her singular goal.

Only the way he looked at her, all banked heat and frustration, and the sparks that crackled in the air every time they spoke, like swordplay, made her all too sure she was not going through it alone.

"There," said Fitz. "Now you're getting it."

Mack's gaze swung to his, terrified she'd said all that out loud, only to realise he meant her seat. Having stopped trying so hard to move with the horse, she now simply was. Not perfectly by any means, but at least she was no longer fighting it.

"Well, look at me go!" she said on a laugh of pure satisfaction.

"Now she wants me to look," Fitz said, leaning forward as if talking to his horse, before shooting her a dark half-smile that did things to her insides she knew she'd be revisiting later.

By mid-morning, temperature rising steadily, Fitz angled them along a route that led to a line of grey gum trees dropping curling ribbons of pink and green bark along the banks of a low river. They slowed as they came upon a waterhole. Dragonflies hovered over the still water. A rock wallaby on the opposite bank lifted its head, sniffed the air then hopped away.

When Mack spied the remnants of an old tyre swing rocking lazily over the water from the branch of a strong unwieldy looking tree, she wondered if it was a place he and his brothers had come when younger. Only to find herself surprised when he said:

"We used to come down here a lot as kids. There was a tree-house, right there." He pointed into the branches overhead. "We'd hide here when we found out Mrs. McRae, our housekeeper, was making tripe. Played poker using Tom's coin collection—he was livid when he found out. Had my first kiss up there—Margot McLaughlin, from School of the Air camp."

His voice trailed off, and Mack's story radar went nuts.

Questions: Was he *offering* her a family angle for the story? Or had the ease of the ride loosened his tongue? Was Margot McLaughlin still on the scene? If not, was there anyone else?

Not that it was any of her business, or relevant to the piece she was writing in any way. Meaning, with a chatty Fitz King on the hook, she surprised the heck out of herself in saying: "Are we on the record?"

Fitz looked over his shoulder; his horse's tail swished at a fly bothering its flank. "Sorry?"

She had *never* done that before. Ever. Once the "rules" had been set, her ethical boundaries locked into place, it was not her job to remind her subject to be careful. It was her job to get the story within those confines.

Yet she'd done it now. "Are you talking to Mackenzie Lawler right now, or me?"

"Aren't you one and the same?"

"Yes, but also no," she admitted, the way he looked at her, with open curiosity now, making her blood thrum. So used was she to feeling as if she was a blank page still to be written on, rather than a story of her own, she wasn't sure what to do with that.

"How does that work?" he asked, hands loosely crossed over the pommel of his saddle, body shifting easily with every movement of the beast beneath him.

He cut such an arresting figure, giving more myth than man, if that moment was the first image on her story, *The Pulse* clicks would break records.

"Mackenzie is always on the clock," she managed. "I'm… Well, I am too, to be honest. So, you make a fair point."

Fitz's gaze roved over her face, as if he could read every thought.

"Mmm," he finally said. "We're a few hours in now. How about all of you clock off for the rest of today."

Her laughter caught on the back of her throat as she wondered if that was even possible. But since he'd requested it, according to her rules, she had to try.

A warm silence hovered over them, bringing with it a shift of purpose, and Fitz leaned back in the saddle as he said, "You mentioned your brother, earlier."

"Half-brother," she corrected. Owning the uncomfortable truth of her family situation was the best way she'd found to move through it as quickly as possible.

"*Half-brother*," Fitz conciliated. "Any other siblings?"

She shook her head. No other blood relatives at all, in fact. "Just Crispin." Then, "You have four brothers, correct?"

A shadow flashed across his eyes. "Most people would say three."

Fitz was smart enough to figure she'd researched him before arriving, so prevaricating for politeness's sake felt disingenuous. "You were how old when your twin brother passed? Ten?"

"Nine."

"And his name was Will?"

Fitz nodded.

"Was he much like you?"

"Not much," he said, his voice low. Then he closed one eye and squinted out into the distance as if beginning to question himself for bringing any of it up at all.

Mack, on the other hand, wasn't ready to lose this whorl of connection blooming between them, for it was a rare happenstance in her experience. "I was twelve when I lost my mother. It's a special kind of loneliness, I think, losing your anchor so young."

"Twelve," he repeated, making a pained sound in the back of his throat. "Crispin didn't step up? Become your new anchor?"

"Crispin is sixteen years older than I am, and

had already left home by the time he even knew I existed. I was the result of a short-lived affair between his father and my mother. When my mother died, very suddenly, and I had no other family to go to, Sir Maximillian's phenomenally forgiving wife, Deanna, took me in."

Fitz curled a hard hand over his reins, his brow hard as he listened. Really listened.

So, Mack went on. "My father on the other hand, not so benevolent. My mother had told me he was a prince from a faraway land, too busy fighting dragons to visit, which at six had made absolute sense. At twelve finding out that he was *not* a dragon-fighter had been a reprieve—who doesn't love a dragon? But the realisation that he'd simply not wanted to know me… That didn't change *after* I moved into Lawler House. I saw him more in the couple of years at work before he died than the entire time I lived in his home."

Fitz, good man, just took it all in. While she claimed to be non-judgemental with her subjects, it took effort. With Fitz it seemed to be true.

"I can't imagine being a kid on my own," he said. "My brothers and I were one living breathing mass of boyhood. All scuffed knees and headlocks and sword fights and pranks, we were a wall of noise for sixteen hours a day, before falling into bed filthy and exhausted."

"That sounds…terrifying." And absolutely wonderful.

Her favourite memories of her childhood were

her mother coming home to their one-bed basement flat in Putney Vale, thanking the lovely upstairs neighbour who babysat most evenings after school, turning on the kitchen radio, then sneaking into their tiny shared bedroom to ask for stories of Mack's day till she fell asleep.

Mack's hand lifted to rub at the sudden ache behind her ribs, only to feel lumps in the pocket of her overalls. The silver-wrapped chocolate Fitz had given her, the exact same kind she'd tossed into her bag the night of the ball, when a sugar hit had been required lest she faint and miss her big moment.

And while she knew it was a risk, pulling a now soft chocolate from the front of her overalls, she said, "I have a little story to tell you."

Fitz cleared his throat, waited for her gaze to find his, then said, "You were at the ball."

"You *knew*?"

The look he gave her was clear—of course he knew. Of course he remembered. While it had only been a moment, it had been a *moment*.

"Why did you not just say so?" he asked.

"I didn't *exactly* have an invitation."

At that, Fitz's eyebrows rose. Turned out he didn't know everything.

Mack waited for the eruption of disappointment or frustration her escapades always brought on. Only the man's head dropped back and he bellowed out a laugh.

"How?" he asked after he collected himself. "Why?"

Relief cascading through her, the story fell from her lips as if it had been waiting for its chance to be set free. When she told him her plan to corner Jackson and charm him into giving her a quote, Fitz's grin was so beautiful it was a miracle she kept her seat.

"I hate to tell you," he said, "but your mission was doomed from the start, as even my brothers and I can barely get a word out of Jack. And yet, the fact you came all this way on a glimmer of hope—respect."

Question: Why was Jackson on the outer with his brothers?

Off the record, and not my story.

"Honestly, I would fully understand if you asked me to leave."

Mack knew she'd seen enough to write a reasonable piece; the rest she could cobble together from testimonials and the website. But where several days ago she'd have jumped at the chance to go home, now the thought of being sent away made something deep inside clench uncomfortably.

She might have a handle on Hideaway Haven, but she wasn't yet done with Fitz King.

Fitz leaned back in the saddle, his horse snuffling, itching to get moving. "That's it then. No more secrets? No more hidden agendas?"

Mack crossed her heart and held up three fingers, which she hoped meant something appropriate.

Fitz breathed out slowly, his expression shifting

through wariness, puzzlement, and something so dark and sensual her stomach turned over on itself in the best way.

Then, voice rough, he asked, "Did you honestly think I'd not remember you?"

Mack's heart whumped, her next breath in hard to come by, and she let her hand slowly drop before saying, "You hid it well enough."

Gaze dropping to her mouth, he shook his head once, then lifted his gaze back to hers and said, "Thought that was for the best."

Mack nodded, even while her heart now beat so hard against her chest she pressed the heel of her palm to the spot, and felt the other chocolates secreted in her overall pocket squishing against her chest.

The chocolate. He knew about the *chocolate*. Meaning he'd seen her, noticed her, was watching her *before* their encounter. She was mighty glad her legs were not in charge of keeping her upright as her knees might just have given way at the thought.

"So, we're good?" she asked.

"We're good."

"Brilliant. And, the whole 'everything beyond the library is out of bounds'—"

"Still stands."

Mack clicked her fingers in mock disappointment.

Fitz chuffed out a laugh, then made a clicking sound and tugged on Yini's reins. The horse turned on a dime and cantered up the small rise leading away from the waterhole, and Mack's horse followed.

"Time to head back," he said when Mack caught up.

"Oh."

Fitz smiled at her patent disappointment. Damn it, she was going to have to be far more careful now. The man didn't miss a thing.

"See those clouds?" he asked, pointing to the east.

Mack looked up and saw. They just looked like clouds to her.

Only by the way he said, "Rain's coming," she didn't argue.

Once they reached the stables, a teen girl took the horses and set to washing them down, after which Fitz drove Mack back to the cabin.

This time he turned off the engine and walked Mack to her door, though his eye was all for the sky. The light morning breeze had become a hot gusty afternoon rush, and now the dusty grey clouds seemed to be rolling over one another on the horizon.

"Satellite phone all charged up?" he asked.

She tapped at her backpack and nodded.

"Stay inside. If rain hits, it'll pass by morning."

"I'm a Londoner. I'm familiar with rain."

"Not the Kimberley kind."

With that he knocked on the wood of the railing, then jogged down the stairs. And with a tip of his hat through the open car window, he took off.

Leaving Mack to wrap her arms about herself, as if she could hold the strange mixed feelings of release and newfound tightness in her chest as long as she could.

Then a blast of hot wind swept up the stairs, and she went inside.

Where, upon sorting through her rations, she found a treasure in the form of Yorkshire Gold tea, the very best tea in all the lands.

She laughed out loud. Rain or no, the gods had been smiling on her that day, for sure.

When Fitz reached the homestead, he saw Tom and Charlie's ute parked at an angle out front, as if they'd driven up, pulled on the handbrake, and opened the door to let Bea fly.

Dammit, he'd forgotten to message Tom back, to explain that there was a journalist on-site. One whose pretty hazel eyes lit up like Christmas any time she heard something that intrigued her.

Not that he'd have told Tom he thought Mack's eyes were pretty, or Mack for that matter, though he'd told her a hell of a lot of things out there by the waterhole. As if there was a little lingering magic in the place. Or maybe it was Will who'd been nudging him to get over himself and talk.

Fitz let himself in through the front door of the homestead, then followed the sound of voices to find Tom, Charlie, and the family's long-time housekeeper, Mrs. McRae, in the large family kitchen.

"Hey," he said, slowing and sliding his hands into the pockets of his jeans. The same stilted reticence coming over him that always hit when his brothers visited from the city. And a marked change from the ease he'd felt talking with Mack.

"Hey, Fitz," said Charlie, who was making sandwiches at the bench, even while Mrs. McRae kept trying to shoo her away.

Tom, checking for homemade snacks in the fridge, cried, "Fritzy!" An old nickname whose origin only Tom would remember. "Good to see you, mate."

Fitz was saved by a loud, "Uncle Fitthhh!"

Fitz turned right as a moppet of five years came whirling at him like the Tasmanian Devil. He braced himself just in time as she slammed into his leg, hanging on tight.

"Buzzy Bea. How are you, kiddo?"

"Good. I loththⁿ a tooth."

"You loth…oh, you lost a tooth."

Through a mouthful of chocolate brownie, Tom said, "Walked into a wall with a bucket on her head while pretending to be Darth Vader. Kununurra dentist says she'll be gappy for a while, and I attest five is still the perfect age for *Star Wars*."

"For you!" said Bea, jumping up and down in front of Fitz to regain his attention. When she handed him a vibrant red friendship band, he slid it on his wrist, beside the last one she'd made for him.

"Did you get *me* a prethent?" Bea asked.

He remembered the silver-wrapped chocolates still left in the pantry, fished out the box, and handed it to her. Bea shrugged, then ran off to check on her succulents.

"Got the kid a pony," Fitz muttered, "and that's all I get."

"Maybe a puppy for Christmas?" Mrs. McRae suggested.

Charlie, coming at Fitz with a Vegemite sandwich and a hug, said, "Don't you dare."

Fitz fell back into his usual role of quiet observer, while Tom, Charlie, and Bea made noise and mess and made Mrs. McRae incandescently happy.

In the past such scenes pressed deeply into old bruises, feeling who was missing more than enjoying those who were there. But compared with Mack's childhood, growing up without any siblings to create any memories alongside, he appreciated that this was good.

Then the room went dark as if a heavy cloud had crossed beneath the sun, and as one the brothers moved to the window in the sunroom off the kitchen and frowned. The gums beyond the back fence were swaying, the sky in the not-too-distant east had taken on a greenish tinge.

"Ominous," said Tom.

"Mmm," Fitz agreed.

"Can we find some time to talk tonight?" Tom asked, moving on.

Fitz nodded, but his mind was elsewhere.

There were two seasons in the far north—wet and dry. When the rain came, bone dry riverbeds could flood, plains that a week before had been grass and trees became inland lakes, roads disappeared from one day to the next, and many of the local cattle stations could find themselves cut off for weeks, even months.

While they weren't there yet, storms in the lead-up could be sudden and violent. He'd felt the signs in the rising humidity, the crackle in the air. Yet rather than tracking it as carefully as he usually would, he'd been distracted by other things. Or, one other person, to be precise. The same person he'd just left in a small cabin in the path of said storm.

The lodgings had been built on sites chosen specifically for their safety and accessibility, and built to last.

Mack was right, she'd be fine.

Dammit.

"Back in a sec," Fitz said to the group at large, as he pulled out his phone, left the kitchen, and made a call.

CHAPTER SIX

"THIS IS ALL a bit exciting," said Julian.

The man had climbed K2 and worked on Wall Street, but apparently waiting to welcome a small group of strangers into Fitz's family home was a thrill.

Fitz, on the other hand, wondered what the hell had come over him. He made a point of *never* asking favours of his father. The Haven paid more than its fair share for leasing the land it used, all tied up in a tight contract keeping things as separate as they could legally be for a reason. This would come at a price.

Once the decision had been made, they'd put out calls to all wilderness guides with the offer to come in. Most were keen to stay put. Caleb, looking after an adventure group at The Rise, had laughed at the prospect. Time was Fitz would have been the same—itching to see what kinds of extremes he could handle. Anything to drown out the chaos that had filled the gap left by Will.

Here, back home, his prime instinct was to keep those he cared about close, and safe. Which, apparently, maddeningly, included Mack Lawler.

A tumble of noise outside heralded the arrival of their "guests," reminding Fitz of the CWA meetings his mother had hosted in the living room, grand Sunday lunches with local station owners, School of the Air kids converging for winter campouts. Since she'd gone the house had gone quiet. Until the night of the ball.

"We managed to keep the team building group in Broome," Julian said, cutting into his thoughts, "comping them a night at the Eco Lodge Resort. So that leaves the Grosvener family of upstate New York, the newlyweds from Melbourne, and the journalist."

As if they had been announced, through the door came a couple, laughing as they shucked off their boots. Then the family—the young teenagers squealing as fat drops of rain began to batter the porch.

And lastly, in walked Mack.

Fitz had spent time with her in the barn, the stables, the front driveway, the waterhole, even his mother's library, but seeing her walk through the front door of his family home, looking clean and fresh and lovely in a floaty dress and sandals the same nut brown as her hair, something shifted inside of him.

Mack laughed as she took the soft towel Julian handed her. Then her eyes searched the small crowd till they found his, and her smile shifted, turning soft, and pleased, and personal.

She slid past the chattering group and idled up

to where Fitz stood. "Is this normal?" she asked, towelling water droplets from her hair.

"The rain or the influx of people into the homestead?"

"Both?"

"The rain, yes," he said, gaze roving over her long, spiked lashes, the high shine of her cheeks, adventure and upheaval suiting her. Or, more likely, he was projecting, wanting it to be true. "People, not so much."

"Then why now?"

She looked up when he'd not answered the question. Then, canny as she was, at the deep fill of his chest as he reminded himself to breathe, she figured it out.

"Oh," she said on a soft breath, pink popping into the highs of her freckled cheeks.

"We need to get you a stronger sunscreen," he murmured, lifting his hand as if about to swipe his thumb across her cheek bone, only to stop himself just in time.

Julian called, "Righty-ho, Haven crew!" and Mack looked his way.

Like a marionette whose strings had been cut, Fitz slumped. He needed to get a grip. Yes, he was extremely attracted to her, and she'd made little effort to hide the fact she wasn't immune to him either. But her job made her a danger to his family's private business, and she was leaving for the other side of the world in a little over a week. He needed to wrest back control before he did something truly stupid, like put himself in a position to miss her.

"We'll show you all to your rooms," said Julian. "Then tonight, the wonderful Mrs. McRae will put on a light dinner, we'll play games, host a talk about local wildlife for the young and young at heart. If the power goes out, do not worry, the homestead has generators so it'll start right back up in seconds."

Mack took a step towards the group as they followed Julian up the stairs, but after all Fitz had done to see her safe, the thought of her disappearing for the night had him reaching out and touching her wrist.

Her gaze shot to the contact, then back up—filled to the brim with questions, and awareness, and heat.

"Come," he said, his voice rough.

When she looked back at the departing Haven crowd, Fitz slid his fingers past the smooth plane of her wrist, past her skittering pulse, to her hold her hand.

Her palm was soft against his callouses, her fingers cool and delicate, and the whole of it fit inside his big mitt as if made to be there.

When she gave him the lightest squeeze, he tugged.

Mack sat at the bench of the King family kitchen, the out-of-bounds part of his home, after having been invited. Watching the lively interplay between Fitz, his brother Tom, soon to be sister-in-law Charlie, and niece Bea, she'd tried not to draw attention lest Fitz realise his error and send her away.

"I've given them a heads up as why you're here," Fitz had said as he'd led her down the hall, leaning down so his words brushed against the lobe of her ear, before slipping his hand from hers and ushering her into the kitchen with a light hand at her lower back. "Whatever happens in this room is as off the record as off the record can be."

"If you insist," she'd countered, attempting levity, though it had come out shakily as she battled the thousand different sensations fighting for one-upmanship inside her, at the whisper of his breath against her skin, the burr of his voice, the fact he had held her hand.

Held. Her. Hand.

Even now she could feel the heat of it, the protective curl of his fingers, the imprint of his tough palm against hers.

Mack was certain no man she'd dated had held her hand before. Not her charismatic senior year boyfriend, nor her charmer of an Oxford beau, or any of the lads she'd dated since.

Maybe that was the key right there—the fact she gravitated towards men she knew would disappoint her, so that when it ended, she could say, "See!" and walk away feeling absolved, rather than heartbroken that once again she'd been let down.

Fitz wasn't like that. He was self-contained, private, protective, and not the type to dally. At least not without it being understood from the outset. So, while the hand-hold seemed such a simple thing, it had been startling in its intimacy.

"What do you think, Mack?"

Mack blinked at Tom. "Sorry, you caught me daydreaming."

"About Hideaway Haven," Tom repeated. "Wildly impressive, right?"

Right. The Haven. The only reason she was there at all. "You'll just have to read the article when it comes out."

"She's good," said Tom, poking a thumb her way.

"Tell me about it," Fitz rumbled, watching her. Smiling at her. *Enjoying* her.

She narrowed her eyes at him, and he did the same back, the connection between them crackling across the room. Add the warmth created by so much affable laughter, and the kind of boisterousness and affectionate teasing Mack had only wished for growing up, and it was a heady feeling indeed.

"Perry and the station crew happy with the storm prep?" asked Tom. Fitz gave him a thumbs-up.

Charlie came around to Mack's side of the bench and sat. "They'll have tied down anything near the house that might be picked up by high wind."

"We got a trampoline for Christmas one year,"

Tom added. "Storm sent it flying across a paddock, busting a horse fence along the way."

"Logan's birthday," Fitz corrected.

"Christmas," Tom disagreed.

"They'll be at it a while now," said Charlie, rolling her eyes indulgently at Tom as he attempted to put Fitz in a headlock with zero luck. "Big fan of your writing, by the way."

Mack turned to face her. "*My* writing?"

"I loved your series matching true crime podcasts with classic novels. Intellectual but accessible. Great stuff."

"Oh," said Mack, genuinely taken aback. "That's so nice to hear." Then, "So you're a regular at *The Pulse*." Her disbelief must have been patent, as Charlie smiled knowingly, and Mack's cheeks grew hot.

"It's tough work, running a station. Heading home for a bubble bath and a scroll of *The Pulse* is restorative," Charlie explained. Then, when Bea started tugging on Tom's jeans, she hopped up, grabbed Bea around the middle, and spun her about the room, so the brothers could talk.

Leaving Mack to absorb Charlie's words. She'd always seen *The Pulse* as lightweight, insubstantial when compared with the hard-hitting lens of *The Indicator*. But the writers still worked just as tirelessly as their upstairs counterparts, so to know that for their audience it had intrinsic and not insignificant value felt rather lovely.

A flicker at the sunroom windows caught

Mack's eye, only with the King men arguing good-naturedly, and Bea and Charlie singing some song about bananas and pyjamas, no one else seemed to notice. When the rumble of thunder rolled over the house, rattling the glassware, they all turned and looked towards the sky.

"Here we go," said Charlie.

"It might be quite the show tonight," said Tom, tickling Bea to keep her distracted from the next bout of thunder.

Fitz, who had moved in behind Mack, said gently, "It also might end up a whole lot of sound and fury, signifying nothing."

Still Mack flinched when fork lightning streaked across the sky with such breadth and violence the rest of them let out a collective, "Oooooh."

And then came the rain. A rising roar that came on fast, before a torrential downpour, silver grey sheets pummelling the earth and drowning out the view.

"Where's Grandad?" cried Bea, as she skipped around the adults, clearly having seen such wild storms before.

"Good question," Tom called back. Then, frowning at Fitz, he said, "Haven't seen him since we arrived."

"Let's go find him," said Charlie, holding out a hand to Bea.

"Wait." Bea trotted back to Mack, dragging something over her wrist.

"For me?" said Mack, as a slightly sticky, lightly

used green and gold friendship band dropped into her hand.

"Yyyyup!" said Bea, before she skipped away.

Charlie, far too astute for Mack's liking, gently squeezed her shoulder, then followed Bea out of the room.

It was such an innocent token of acceptance, but to Mack it felt like so much more. It was this house, and the ribald, intelligent mess of memories held within its walls; bittersweet proof that money and success could be a wholesome means of connection in some families.

It was the man asking, "You alright?"

Mack glanced up to find Fitz smiling down at the tatty strings she'd tied around her wrist while he played with the two sets he now wore tucked up against his watch.

"Yes," she said, though her throat felt uncomfortably tight. "I'm great. Just… I should leave you boys to catch up. So nice to meet you, Tom. Good night." With that she fled the room.

She was also unsurprised when Fitz followed.

When she reached the bottom of the grand staircase, she squared her shoulders and turned to face him, readying to make it clear that next time they spoke, he'd better be ready for a barrage of tough, entirely non-personal questions.

Instead, she found herself saying, "Your family is lovely. Thank you for allowing me to meet them."

"That wasn't for the story—"

She held up both hands. "I know. Off the record. Not a word."

"No, I meant…" He took a moment to choose his words. "I thought you'd like to meet them, and knew they'd like to meet you."

Mack blinked, for that was one of the sweetest things anyone had ever said to her. Before she could stop herself, she stepped in, placed a slightly trembling hand against his chest, lifted up onto her toes, and kissed Fitz King on the cheek.

The rough press of his jaw, the deep sun-drenched warmth of his skin, and the earthy scent of the man—he was a sensory overload. Like how it felt to step out of her cabin as the sun first touched the land beyond, times a hundred.

Nerves singing, apprehensive at how quickly things seemed to be developing now, she dropped back to the flats of her feet, turned on wobbly legs and flew up the stairs to find Julian, so she could find her room and lock herself away for the rest of what was sure to be a long night.

Fitz watched Mack head upstairs, rubbing a hand over the place her fingers had curled. He'd leaped from cliff tops, hauled himself up sheer rock faces without a safety rope, free dived through caves as dark as deep space, but nothing stole his breath the way Mack Lawler could.

"Everyone settled in?"

Fitz spun to find his father strolling down the

hall, likely having just come out from his personal office along the way.

Clearing his throat, Fitz said, "I believe so."

Hands in the pockets of clean chinos, his father had clearly showered off the usual layer of red dirt and sweat in honour of their guests. Tall and imposing, grey-tinged hair swept back off his face, the man looked dapper as hell. For all that his father was a farmer to the marrow, when it came to being the public face of the King family, he could still switch it on.

"Sorry, one last thing—*oh.*"

Fitz stilled, then turned to find Mack had come back down the stairs.

Her cheeks were flushed as if she'd jogged the whole way. Or, considering the buzz of inquisitiveness zapping around her like a mosquito catcher on a summer's night, because she'd just landed herself an audience with Fraser King.

"Well, hello, there," said his father, voice dropping, eyes twinkling as he turned on the Outback Aussie charm.

Fitz gave his father a look, before moving to stand by Mack, unsure in that moment as to who needed his protection more.

"Mack," said Fitz, "this is my father, Fraser King. Dad, this is Mackenzie Lawler. A journalist from *The Pulse* in London. She is here to write an article about Hideaway Haven."

He'd yet to confront his father about how it had come about, but the way Fraser said, "Ah," and rocked back on his heels was the closest Fitz had ever come to seeing the man expressing chagrin.

Mack, being Mack, ate up every second of it, before saying, “Mr. King, you are so kind letting us stay here till the storm passes. I had assured Fitz that as a Londoner I wasn’t afraid of a little rain, but from all I’ve seen of your property so far, you don’t do things by halves out here.”

Fraser’s chin lifted. “In a place like the Kimberley, one has to step up to match the landscape or it’s all over before you’ve begun.”

“Mmm.”

“Now,” said Fraser, leaning in, “how has your stay at Fitz’s little resort been so far?”

Fitz felt the air turned a degree cooler, and he remembered calling her notebook *little* back on day dot. He’d been needling her to cover his surprise at seeing her again, but the way she’d refused to take it lying down had been magnificent.

When he felt her rev up again, this time to defend *him*, he lay a gentle hand on her back. After a beat, she leaned back into his touch, showing him that she understood.

Then, she smiled sweetly and said, “I know more about sunscreen and spinifex grass than I had imagined I would.”

Fraser laughed. Charmed to pieces.

But rather than shooting her shot and hitting Fraser with her best question right when she had him, she said, “And now I can’t remember why I came back down here.”

Fitz, giving her the out, said, "If you do later, come find me."

"Will do."

As one the King men watched her walk back up the steps, all bounce and light. And while imagining all the reasons why she might have come looking for him would keep him up half the night, keeping her away from his father, and vice versa, was the lesser evil.

Power flickered through the house, and the sensor night lights Tom had had added to the hallway floor after Bea was born turned on. And Fitz looked to his father, to find that without Mack to charm, the lights in his eyes had turned low.

Conflicting emotions scuttled through Fitz, all of which he struggled to reconcile. His hero worship as a kid twisted after the blame his brothers had thrown their father's way. His father's introversion that once balanced perfectly with his mother's extroversion now made him shuttered and hard to know. The man's deep pride in the history of the family, and the house, both were teetering on the verge of becoming anachronisms.

But then a record started playing in the library, Tom, Charlie, and Bea could be heard singing along, and his father came to. "I assume this means you're sleeping here tonight too?"

Here, meaning his childhood suite. Rooms he'd once upon a time shared with Will. "Considering the elements, I'd say that's the best option."

"The elements, is it?" Fraser asked, mouth hitching at one corner as he glanced back up the stairs.

Then with that Fraser tipped an imaginary Akubra, walked back to his private office, and, as usual, shut the door behind him.

CHAPTER SEVEN

It was well after midnight before the house finally settled.

After dinner and games, with the visitors all tucked up in their well-appointed rooms, Ned and Julian ran back to the cottage, grabbing their chance to have it to themselves for a night.

Tom had long since carried a sleeping Bea up the stairs to his private suite, Charlie's head tipped onto his shoulder. And while Fitz was happy for Tom, he didn't understand how his brother didn't spend every waking minute feeling as if his heart was beating outside his chest, waiting for the bad thing that would take it all away.

Doing a final check of the house, and finding excuses not to head to his own suite, Fitz ended up at the library when he heard music playing.

There he found Mack curled up on a single-seater couch in the corner, dark hair spilling over the arm of the chair, Ella Fitzgerald on the record player. And while the storm raged outside, she was fast asleep.

She made a small noise, and one of the cushions

under her head slipped free. Fitz reached down to catch it, right as she snuffled awake.

Eyes blinking open to find him a mere foot away, her lashes made gentle sweeps against sleep-pinkened cheeks. “Fitz,” she breathed, her mouth curling into a smile of pure delight.

Fitz’s heart whumped so hard in his chest he worried it might be the last whump it ever whumped.

“You’re in your PJs,” she said, her gaze skipping from the colum of his throat to the fit of his soft shirt, to the unforgiving fall of pajama pants as if it didn’t know where to land.

“As are you,” he said.

Blinking sleepily, she looked down to see she was in a neck-to-ankle nightgown, the kind Fitz imagined Victorian woman might have worn. Not that he imagined Victorian women nearly as much as he imagined this one.

“So I am,” she said in the breathiest of voices, at which point she realised she was curled up on a chair. In the library. In the middle of the night.

Untangling herself from the tight spot, she stood, her bare feet curling over one another. “Sorry, I figured since you’d given me permission to be here before you would not mind, and I wasn’t keen on the big tree swaying wildly right outside my bedroom window—”

“Mack,” he said, his hand outstretched, his fingers tingling from knowing how close they were to the shadow of her fine collarbone, the fall of her silken hair, the freckles dusting her skin.

"Yes?"

"It's fine."

"Oh. Well, that's good."

If his voice had been low and rough, hers was whisper quiet. He had to strain to hear it over the storm. That was excuse enough to move closer. Close enough she had to raise her chin to meet his eyes. Close enough for him to see her pupils darkening, the trembling that had nothing to do with the cool of the night.

He knew, because he felt it too. Like a shimmer that began in his chest and radiated outwards, it felt like inevitability.

Then her gaze dropped to his mouth and she licked her lips.

"Mack," he said again, and whatever she heard in his voice told her enough, for she took the next step, and her arms were around his neck, his around her waist, and he'd lifted her off the ground.

And they were kissing. Kissing. *Kissing.*

As if their very lives depended on it. As if the storm heralded end of days and this was their one chance to do all the things they'd been imagining they might do since the night they met.

Her hands were in his hair, sliding, gripping. One of her legs hooked around his as best it could while tangled in all that fabric.

And her mouth, good gods that mouth.

She tasted of mint and fresh air and peril. And while he knew that in giving in to this compulsion he was playing with fire, in that moment with her soft body clinging to him, her mouth opening for him, he'd burn for her if that's what she asked of him.

"Wait," she whispered against his mouth, gently touching her forehead to his. "I don't know if we should..."

Fitz softened his hold, and he waited. Felt as if he'd been waiting for this for longer than he even knew. Even while the tremors he'd felt watching Tom and Charlie lean on one another began to leach into the edges of his mind.

Then with a moan, Mack's chin dipped and her lips brushed over his. Like a whisper. Like a promise.

He slid a hand up into her hair and held her there. Licks of heat flashed through his veins at the soft sounds of pleasure she made as his tongue traced the seam of her lips, then swept luxuriously into her mouth.

When they next came to, Mack's hand was deep in his hair, her nightgown bunched at her back in his tight fists, and the both of them breathed in great clumps of air. Her head dropped backwards, a groan falling from her lips at the madness that had infected them both. It took Fitz a while longer to climb out of what felt like a drug-induced haze.

"Holy moly," she said. "That was something."

"I'll say," he said, while quietly thinking this

woman was his own personal fork lightning, shooting across his sky in a way that would not be denied.

While she shivered, as if even his voice set her off. “Maybe…maybe since we are both here, both rather wide awake, we can continue our interviews?”

Fitz huffed out a ragged laugh. Only Mack Lawler would attempt to cool things down by resuming work.

“If you wish,” he said, gently lowering her. Holding on to sanity by the skin of his teeth when she shivered at the unavoidable feel of his erection against her belly.

When her feet touched the ground, he wasn’t ready to lose the feel of her in her arms. He bunched her dress a little tighter, and a little higher, till she melted against him, her knee nudging between his, sending shooting stars across his vision.

“What is it that you wish to ask me, Ms. Lawler?” he asked, slowly bending her over his arm and brushing his lips over her ear.

“Ask?” she whispered, letting her head fall back. “I can’t think. Maybe…what’s your favourite colour?”

Fitz’s mouth cocked into a grin. “Right now?” he said, running his nose over her collarbone. “Pale pink. You?”

Lifting her back upright, like a slow motion dance, Fitz lifted the fabric with one hand, and slid the other lower till his fingertips met the skin at the back of her thighs.

When he ran his hand down her leg then up again, his thumb brushing the curve of her backside, her head fell to rest against his chest. "What was the question again?"

Fitz didn't give a damn as his fingers found the edge of her underwear, curling millimetres beneath, only to realise how close they were to tipping over into something more. In the library. While a dozen other people slept in the house above.

That finally brought back a sliver of sense, and with a big breath out, Fitz slowly let the fabric bunched in his hand drop back to the floor.

"Storm's abating," he rumbled against her hair, as he smoothed the fabric over her back. "Time to get some sleep."

Mack nodded. "Sensible decision. Good idea."

They held one another for a few long moments, fingers tracing circles over one another's back, toying with one another's hair, knees sliding over and between, before they disentangled themselves. And he felt the loss of her warmth like the first warning pulse of a toothache.

"Ladies first," he said, motioning to the door.

Mack caught his eyes, hers dancing, her mouth biting back a smile. Then, shaking off one final shiver, she moved to the door, checked the way was clear, then flapped her hand, beckoning him to follow.

Fitz would never have thought he'd one day find himself mirroring the night of the ball, yet here they were, skulking the hallways of the homestead on soft feet, ear pricked for company, before they jogged up the stairs as if a devil was at their heels.

Fitz followed as she hooked a left towards the guest suites and they pulled up, puffing slightly when they reached an open doorway.

"This is you?" he asked. Glancing inside, he saw Mack's brown dress tossed haphazardly onto the corner of her unmade bed. He pictured her undoing each button, the fabric sliding over her pale skin, her feet stepping out of the puddle of fabric, leaving her standing in the moonlight in nothing but—

"Prepare yourself, Fitz King," she said.

And he snapped back to the present, to find her holding the back of her hand to her mouth as she gave in to a small yawn. "Now I've wheedled your favourite colour out of you, my plan is to get you to admit your favourite day of the week."

Whatever today is, he thought. Then, letting the recklessness that had once upon a time hummed just below the surface of all he did take point, he slid his hand to her jaw, angling it the way he wanted, his thumb running over her cheekbone.

Then, stepping in, holding her just so, he leaned down, kissed her, long, deep, slow, mind-bending, holding nothing back.

When he pulled back, Mack swayed on her feet and grabbed him by the shirt front as if it was the only thing keeping her upright. A good ten seconds later her eyes opened. Languidly. As if it was the last thing they wanted to do.

"Good night, Mack," said Fitz, dragging his gaze from her lovely face to glance pointedly at her bedroom door.

"Good night?" she returned, the rising note of a question all too clear.

Fitz, holding on to his very last modicum of sense, kissed the tip of her nose and let his hand slide from her cheek.

Then, with a curse that came as more of a growl, he left her there and went to sleep in the room he'd not slept in since he was a child.

Mack woke feeling the warm, gooey, deliciousness that came from a brilliant night's sleep. Stretching out like a starfish, she blinked up at a high ceiling with beautiful mouldings and a vintage pendant light and thought, *Huh.*

She travelled so much for work she often had to look at her weather app to remember where she was. But as golden light played across the ceiling, sunshine dappling the walls through the leaves of the big gum tree outside her room, she remembered it all.

Scrambling to sit up, her head swam and her fingers flew to her lips. For, oh my, the kissing. The man's hands in her nightgown, his breath on her neck. His calloused fingers curving around the edge of her underwear…

Pressing her knees together as heat pooled between her thighs, she let her face fall into her palms.

What have I done? And what to do now?

Lifting her head, she looked unseeingly across the room. She'd been clear from the outset her article would be nothing but positive, so that was not a concern, and while the night before had been unanticipated, it was hardly criminal. Neither, come to that, was her dash across the globe the first time. If she'd come back from Kings Reach having successfully nabbed a quote she'd have been labelled plucky, a maverick, a *Lawler.* Instead, she'd been made to feel as if her very career was at stake.

And yet…

For all that Crispin, and *The Indicator* for that matter, could be rather stuffy and lacked appreciation for her zest, his assertion that she made a habit of getting in her own way was not wrong.

Yes, Fitz King was made up of infinite layers she could happily spend days unwrapping, but her mission, her number one focus had to be the story. Getting entangled would only mean a whole lot of awkward disentangling at the end, and with Fitz she'd not get the comfort of the "See!" moment when it was all over. For while he could be a grouch, and frustratingly stubborn, there was not a disappointing bone in his body.

Time to face the music, the man, and probably a slew of semi-strangers with whom she'd played G-rated charades the night before, Mack showered and dressed, packed her small overnighter, then headed downstairs.

Finding no one about, she followed voices, turning into the family kitchen and…

Fitz.

The man made her blood fizz at the best of times, but now, after having his hands on her, knowing he kissed as if he'd been let off a leash, his name spun through her like a cartwheel and a sigh.

Leaning against the kitchen bench, espresso cup in hand, the sleeves of his checkered button-down rolled to his elbows, faded jeans hugging the hard planes of his thighs, the man looked like a poster for clean country living. While his stubble, now long enough it had begun to curl, made her lips tingle with the memory of how it had felt to kiss him with that little bit of rough, her thoughts were anything but clean.

She must have made a sound, as Fitz looked up and stood taller upon seeing her. But his gaze was dark, unreadable.

"Morning," she managed to say, even as her fingers tingled with the memory of how it had felt to run them through his hair.

Fitz gave her the most infinitesimal nod in response, then drank his coffee. Then he rinsed his cup and put it in the dishwasher, and it was a miracle she didn't moan out loud.

Should she simply say it? Make it clear that,

while perfectly lovely, their dalliance in the library probably shouldn't happen again. Probably.

Instead, when his gaze snagged on hers, and her pulse went haywire, she went with, "What's the plan for today?"

After a long beat, Fitz looked to the watch hanging loosely on his solid wrist, the friendship bands his adorable niece had made him entangled alongside it. "As soon as you're packed and ready, Sinclair will drive you back to The Ridge."

Mack blinked, running his words over in her head a second time. *Sinclair will drive me back?*

Right, well, maybe she didn't have to say anything at all. For he was clearly on the same page. Like the storm the night before, they'd had a build-up of chemistry, which the kiss had broken, and now it was back to work.

Brilliant.

"Right!" she said, keeping it bright and cheerful. "I guess I'm ready now."

"I'll let her know." Fitz slid his phone from the back pocket of his jeans. Tapping away, he added, "Anything else you'd like to do today, let her know. Keep in mind, tomorrow we ship you out to The Rise."

So soon? Mack thought, clearly having lost track of her days. And from what she'd read, The Rise was a long way from the homestead, meaning unless Fitz chose to come out to see her, their in-person interviews were at an end.

And the last thing she'd asked of him had been his favourite colour.

Definitely ready now to make it clear their torrid evening was one and done, Mack was stymied by Charlie bustling into the kitchen with Bea right behind her.

"We're off!" Charlie said. Then, catching sight of Mack, her eyebrows rose. "You're still here."

Mack blinked. "I…am! Another week or so till I head home."

"After the heat here, you won't know yourself."

"I think you're right. The trees were only just starting to turn russet gold when I left, but it'll be properly autumnal by then. It really is the prettiest time of year."

Charlie smiled. But then her expression turned mischievous. "Though by *here*, I meant *here*. The others left an hour ago."

Gaze snapping to Fitz to find him blithely busying himself with some papers on the bench, Mack said, "My fault. I slept in. I was up far too late last night. Regretfully."

Feeling Fitz's gaze narrow at her less than subtle dig, Mack added an imaginary tally score to her side of the ledger.

Then Bea jumped up and down in front of Fitz. "Come *thay* goodbye!"

With a growl, Fitz swept Bea into his arms and flipped her upside down, the girl squealing in delight as he carried her out of the room. And despite a growing desire to give Fitz a shake, there was no denying it was adorable.

When Charlie followed, Mack did the same, only to find Fitz and Bea making their way out the front door.

"He's a pretty good uncle, that one," said Charlie. "Good man too."

Mack hoped the sound she made was noncommittal, even while her organs were now in full conflict inside her. Heart and gut, mind and ovaries, all fighting to be heard.

When they reached the front door, Sinclair stepped inside. "Hey, Mack. You ready?"

Mack baulked, a sudden hollowness filling her up at the thought that that might actually be it. At the possibility that she literally might not see the man again.

Charlie shook her head. "He's also a King, clueless lumps the lot of them. Till they're not." Then she said, "I hope to see you again," and pulled Mack into a quick hug, then was gone.

With the Kings all gone, the large house suddenly held a familiar kind of quiet, the kind that to Mack felt like deep loneliness. Not keen to go down that memory lane, she headed upstairs, gathered her small bag, and met Sinclair back in the foyer.

Sinclair took her out a back door of the house, where a new Land Cruiser awaited. Once Mack was buckled in, they were off, her only glimpse of Fitz saying goodbye to his family as Sinclair drove her away.

Looking frontward, to the vast spread of red dirt, and dry bush, and miles of unmade road——as wildly different from the urban sprawl, and heavy traffic, and conveniences of London as a place could be—Mack knew, in theory, it was the best thing.

Only the flood of disappointment that rose inside her had nothing to do with any inaction on Fitz's part, and everything to do with her own.

CHAPTER EIGHT

THAT EVENING, AS NICKI and Mike—a Kings Reach and Hideaway Haven staffer respectively—were celebrating their fifth wedding anniversary, a party had been organised at the Rec Club, a large new-ish building walking distance from the homestead.

Fitz tended not to attend such events, so the staff could let their hair down. But feeling twitchy as a crow in a cage all damn day, he'd needed something to take his mind off things. "Things" being Mack Lawler. More specifically how it had felt to watch Sinclair drive her away.

He could have taken her back to the cabin. Should have, so that they could address the events of the evening before. But after tossing and turning all night from knowing she was just down the hall, the thought of sitting in the car with her, her scent swirling about him, had felt akin to sadomasochism.

Especially after she'd spoken of home. Her face lighting up as she'd talked to Charlie of the cool, the seasons, some of the many things about her home she no doubt missed. If he'd needed a great big flashing sign that cooling things, or better yet, cutting off their air supply completely, was imperative, that had done it.

Kasey Chambers was pumping from the jukebox, as Fitz arrived at the Rec Club. The pool table and dartboard were getting a workout, and someone had taken it upon themselves to fancy the place up, with fairy lights and balloons hanging from a net tacked to the ceiling. It was a surprise to him that there were nearly as many Hideaway Haven staff there as Kings Reach, all mixing as if they were one big happy family.

Spotting his core staff by the bar, he headed that way.

"Boss!" cried Sinclair, eyes concerned. "Everything alright?"

Fitz motioned to the station hand on bar duty to slide him abeer. "Everything's fine. I'm here for the celebration like everyone else."

"I wonder why?" said Julian, waggling his eyebrows as he glanced across the crowd.

As the crowd parted, the opening notes of "Crazy" by Patsy Cline poured gently from the jukebox, and there, chatting animatedly with Analise and his father, was Mack Lawler.

At least he thought it was Mack. For the woman's hair was a riot of loose curls, dark jeans hugged her from hip to her ankle, her shimmery black top sported wire thin straps that twinkled as she moved, and she wore high heels sharp enough to neuter a man if he did her dirty.

She glanced sideways, and there was no doubt. That was her sweet nose with its smattering of freckles, her lush mouth painted a slick ruby red.

When she asked his father a question and the man answered, chatting away as if they'd known one another for years, Fitz found himself caught between wanting to separate her from his father before the family secrets were all hers, and throwing her over his shoulder and taking her some place private where he could kiss that lipstick off her pretty mouth and leave traces of it all over her body.

Then, as if she'd felt his attention, she stilled, looked across the room and right into his eyes. And she smiled a smile that said, *You handled this morning poorly, and I'm giving you one more chance.*

While the sounds around him faded to a dull roar, his fingers ached and his crotch grew hard at the memory of holding her, fingers tangled in her hair, her knee sliding between his thighs. Hoping to project at least a modicum of self-preservation, Fitz frowned for all he was worth, and lifted his hands in question.

Mack lifted her drink, a tall creamy-looking cocktail with a bright pink umbrella sticking out the top, in salute. All the things he'd left unsaid that morning swelling inside his head, he lifted his beer in return.

Then he turned back to the bar, gripping the cool

wood and thinking of England. Funnily enough, it helped.

"He alright?" Caleb's Irish lilt floated to him.

When Fitz glanced, one-eyed, at his staff, all four were watching him with open enthralment. Till Julian brought up the upcoming test cricket season and they were duly distracted.

"Hello, all." Mack's lilting voice rolled over his skin like a bonfire flare.

Fitz turned, slowly, as the others called back, "Hey, Mack!"

"This place is amazing," she said. "Fraser and Annalise were just telling me how it all came about—the Kings donating the building, the staff creating and managing the co-op. What a brilliant move."

"Nice to have somewhere to blow off steam after a hard week's work," Caleb crooned, flexing as he took a swig.

When the growl in Fitz's chest made it to his throat, Julian gathered the crew and ushered them away.

Then, as if she'd only just noticed him, Mack said, "Fitz. Fancy seeing you here."

"I could say the same about you."

"Fair. But considering I'm about to be shipped off to the wild blue yonder tomorrow, when Annalise invited me, I couldn't say no."

"I did," said Anna, popping out from behind Mack and giving Fitz a sorry-not-sorry smile. "Not often I feel homesick, but hearing that accent I had to steal her for a bit to get some news from home."

"By 'news,'" said Mack, "she means someone with whom to talk *Strictly*."

"*Come Dancing*," Mack and Anna added, laughing in unison, when it was clear Fitz had no clue what they were talking about. Because apparently, they were best friends now.

"You must miss so many things," Mack said, "living all the way out here."

"Such as?" Anna asked.

"Not having a local M&S, for one. What I wouldn't give for a bag of Percy Pigs."

Anna glanced at Fitz and said, "I'd say the only thing I have missed is a good ol' cup of Yorkshire tea."

Mack grabbed Anna's arm. "I have some in my cabin right now."

Anna's eyes widened as she pointed a finger directly at his face. "I knew it! That's why you were asking me about it the other day. You wanted to nab some to help Mackenzie feel more at home."

Fitz looked down at his shoes and breathed deeply.

"Isn't he the sweetest?" Anna asked of Mack.

"Yes," Mack agreed. "The sweetest."

At the raw edge to her voice, Fitz looked up, and the expression on Mack's face told him she was both furious with him and wanted to slide her hands under his shirt immediately. He knew the feeling, intimately.

Eyes on Mack, he said to Anna, "Might my father be wondering where you are?"

Anna, natural earnestness snapping into place, said, "You're right. It's getting late. I really should get him back home." With that, she disappeared into the crowd.

Mack, casually as you please, moved to lean against the bar beside Fitz and looked out over the crowd.

"Having a nice time?" Fitz asked.

"Very much."

"I hope the manners here are not too banal. Or confronting."

Her sharp glance felt like the back of a fingernail stroked down his neck. "I work in news, Mr. King. There is very little that shocks me. And I like how honest people are here. How open, and up for a good chat."

Fitz's jaw clenched. Attempting to lock her down was like trying to lasso lightning, or a firefly at dusk, for she was zap and flitters, constantly at the edge of his vision, illuminating and bedazzling and impossible to capture.

"The art of understatement," she went on, "that those in the Lawler family circle are masters of from birth, is something I've never been able to get the hang of."

Fitz turned to face her. "Are you saying, Ms. Lawler, that you are beginning to like it here?"

"Ever since you brought me the good tea," she

said, turning on him a smile that made him see stars. "Thank you."

"You're welcome."

"Landslide" crooned from the jukebox, and from the corner of his eye he saw couples stray to a makeshift dance floor, and someone dimmed the lights. Mack watched with a small smile on her face, her interest in the gamut of human experience second to none.

Needing an anchor, Fitz asked, "What were you talking to my father about?"

"Hideaway Haven, of course. Your father is terribly proud of what you've achieved here."

Before he could censor himself, Fitz scoffed.

At that Mack finally turned to face him. "Is that really such a surprise?"

Fitz did not want to talk to Mack about his father. And he especially did not want to talk about his father and the Haven in the same breath. He was still working his way through how best to protect his business if the trust was disbanded.

While his brothers might think his reaction had been less impassioned than they'd hoped, considering how hard he'd been known to throw himself at life in the past, but he'd only had himself to think about then. Now he had staff. People who relied on him, and letting emotion rule his head, he'd not been able to protect Will, instead making everything far worse, and he'd damn well not make the same mistake again.

"Fitz?" Mack nudged gently when her usual tactic of leaving quiet for him to fill didn't work.

"How would you answer that question?" he asked.

He'd caught her off guard, but she didn't flinch. "My father and I were both drawn to the same work, we were related by blood, and I did not know the man well enough to know if he was proud of me or not. Can you say the same about yours?"

Fitz attempted to glare her down, but she merely lifted an eyebrow and waited. For she'd made a solid point.

After Will's death, with his brothers blaming Fraser for the accident that had taken his life, his mother had been forced to ameliorate the fury on both sides, all while grieving herself. Leaving Fitz, barely nine years old, to sit at the very centre of the maelstrom—fractured hero worship, secret guilt, and unfathomable loss whipping about him like the loudest winds.

While the scars of that time still pinched when he least expected, he and his father endured one another for the sake of Kings Reach. Yes, it was imperfect, but their uneasy peace was a vast improvement on the before.

Before the ball Fitz had hoped it might continue to move in that direction. Maybe, even now, he still did.

Aware he was about to open a metaphorical vein for this woman, but unable to stop himself,

Fitz murmured, "I wanted to be my father when I grew up."

When Mack could have asked a thousand other things, she gifted him with: "What about him did you love most?"

What had he loved most? About his father? Even with chatter and laughter and music filling the air, Fitz found himself flung back into a time.

"He was so tough," Fitz said. "Undaunted, inviolable, as if born with Kings Reach dirt beneath his fingernails. He had years of family history to lean on, but he also took big swings. His instincts were impeccable, and the respect he garnered from our station hands was patent. He was, for want of a better word, a king."

"And now?" she asked.

A spotlight had been turned on, hitting a disco ball hanging from the centre of the ceiling, and reflected light danced over the crowd like a wave as the bluesy strains of "Tennessee Whiskey" wafted across the room.

Fitz turned to look at Mack. Curiosity ran like a river behind her pretty hazel eyes, yet he did not *feel* as if he was being interviewed by a practised journalist. Being with her, he felt like she was exactly where she was meant to be.

Fitz held out a hand, then cocked his head towards the dance floor.

For the first time that night she looked to be on the back foot, but then she placed her hand in his, the friendship band Bea had given her wrapped about her wrist.

"Come on, Lawler," he said, tucking her hand into the crook of his elbow, needing her close, wanting her right there beside him.

The crowd seemed to give way as they passed, until they stopped in the middle of the club. He spun her out to the end of his arm, then tugged her into a dance hold and began to sway.

Mack breathed out a breathy laugh as her delighted gaze found his. "You, Fitz King, are a constant surprise."

"Nah," he said, tucking their joined hands between them. "I'm just your basic, run of the mill Outback cattleman slash national ecotourism award winner."

"God bless Australia," she said. Then, with a happy hum, she rested her cheek against his shoulder.

They danced that way for a minute, more, before Fitz said, "How do you feel about me being your guide at The Rise next week?"

Mack lifted her head, her gaze bright. "Are you serious?"

"That's one word for it," he said, turning her in a circle to distract from the fact he had pulled her closer still. "Only way I see it that we can hit the ten hours of agreed upon interview time."

"Rules are rules," she agreed, the hand at his shoulder sliding up his neck till her fingers toyed with his hair.

And as the music eddied around them in a lovestruck lament, there was no sidestepping it anymore—Mack Lawler had hit him like a steam train. All he could do now was wait for her to pass on through, then deal with the damage afterwards.

It had rained again overnight, Fitz noted as he let Ranger out for his morning sniff, the kind that barely settled the dust, the damp burning off quickly in the heat of the late spring sun.

He hoped his energy might do the same as it thrummed like an electric current, knowing that in a couple of hours he'd be picking up Mack to drive her out to The Rise. Would she have heard the rain? Would it have felt more like the rain back home, as opposed to the big storm? Why did that suddenly feel important?

Time for coffee.

Fitz looked across to the homestead—every addition and extension a loving nod to its original Federation-style architecture and a historied testament to generations of King family living.

Mack hadn't been the first to question if he'd considered opening the house for cattle station-centric homestays. It was the smart move, what with so many families in the region leaving due to drought, flood, debt, labour shortage, market forces. Fitz's disinclination hadn't been due to fear of failure, or even his father's resistance; he had a profound and persistent awareness that nothing he held dear could be trusted to endure.

It was why his father's bombshell hadn't been near as much of a surprise to him as it had been to the others. That was life, right? When he'd curated the Haven, he'd built in an out. He could take the Haven brand elsewhere, if the need came.

Ironically, now it loomed as an actual possibility, he didn't want to.

The party had made it all too clear that the Haven wasn't just about him anymore. It was Ned and Julian, Caleb and Sinclair, and the dozens of staff who ran the place and relied on him. The Haven and the Reach had become intertwined whether he'd wanted it or not.

Fitz headed to the homestead kitchen for his morning coffee, only to pull up at the sight of his father hunched over at the bench. Usually on the station by now, instead he looked to be reading an agricultural report on the tablet Annalise had set up for him, while eating slow mouthfuls of the porridge with brown sugar he'd had for breakfast every day Fitz had known him.

"Morning, son," said Fraser, without looking back.

"Morning." Fitz headed for the coffee machine. Only, spying leftovers in the saucepan, he filled his own bowl with porridge and leaned against the bench.

He watched his father eat another mouthful and wince. And noted the brown sugar was no more. It had to be Annalise, attempting to get his father on a health kick. No wonder she'd looked so defeated the other morning.

The scrape of his father's chair against the terrazzo tile had Fitz looking up as the older man motioned to the chair beside his. Surprised, Fitz took it.

"Enjoy the party last night?" Fitz asked.

"Was starting to, till a certain someone told Analise to take me home."

"You might want to give her a break, if you want her to stick around."

"Sucker for hard work, that one."

"Have to be, to work for you."

Fraser glanced to Fitz and lifted his spoon in salute. "Well, look who's finally woken up."

"It's after six," Fitz shot back. "I've been awake for an hour."

"Don't be obtuse, son, it doesn't suit you."

Fitz disagreed. Playing the stoic, silent cowboy archetype had people keeping a wide berth, which had suited him just fine.

Fraser's eyes narrowed. "With your seat, and your resilience, you were born to work the land, but I always thought it a shame it hid how shrewd you were. Your mother knew it, practically raising you in that library of hers, but I did always wonder if it passed your brothers by."

Heat crept up Fitz's neck at the twisted compliment. Then he leaned across the bench, reached for the bowl of brown sugar, scooped out a copious amount, scattered it over his porridge, and shovelled a massive spoonful into his smiling mouth.

"I'd ask what the hell's gotten into you," Fraser said, "but I think I know. She's a spitfire, that one. Near impossible to domesticate, but fun to try, if you have the mettle. I should know."

Fitz considered equivocating, but clearly that horse had bolted. Their dance the night before was as good as an announcement that something was in the air. So, instead, Fitz chose directness. "On that subject, what made you think it was okay to invite a journalist to do a write-up on the Haven without consulting me?"

Fraser placed his spoon in his bowl and turned to face Fitz, as if he'd been waiting for this question all week long. "Her brother called me a couple of months back."

Fitz stilled. Her *brother*?

"Said her wheels were spinning and she needed a challenge. Would I be amenable to taking her on for a couple of weeks. Give her something to get her teeth stuck into." His father's brows knitted. "I'm aware Kings Reach is hardly of interest to young people these days. While what you have built here clearly is, considering the numbers of excitable young adults zooming in and out of the place. So, I suggested you."

Mack's voice saying, *Your father is terribly proud of what you've achieved here*, slid into his head, and it stopped him from pressing. The man was making a lot of bold choices without consultation these days, and, to be fair, this was the longest conversation they'd had that did not revolve around water, or fences, or horse management in weeks. Months. Maybe even years.

"How do you even know Crispin Lawler?" Fitz asked.

"I've known him since he was a lad. His father and I ran in similar circles in the old days when your mother and I travelled to the UK, repping Aussie beef. He made a play for her once, at a Britain–Australia Society Australia Day Gala."

At that Fitz coughed out a bark of surprise. Then realised Maximillian Lawler had likely been married at the time, and he felt a burn in his belly for Mack.

His father had made mistakes, but he was the only person in Fitz's inner circle who had never left him, not physically anyway.

"Dad," Fitz said, and damn if his voice didn't come out like a bullfrog before a storm. "Can I ask you about the trust?"

Fraser let his spoon drop to the bowl with a loud clink. "What do you want to know?"

"Why are you doing this? Seriously. Not the bull about it being what mum wanted, as we all know that's not true."

"You know less than you think you do, kid," his father said, pushing back his stool, his face pulling in a way that looked like grief. "Figure it out soon, or let the chips will fall where they may."

With that Fraser walked out the door.

Fitz watched the empty space for a few long moments. While he should have felt as if the ground had been whipped out from under him, again, this time he knew it was no whim—there were machinations at play. And, if he'd read the situation right, there was a way out.

He and his brothers simply had to figure out what the hell that was.

And for some reason, it gave him hope.

CHAPTER NINE

FITZ WAS UNUSUALLY serene on the drive out to The Rise. And while grumpy Fitz was entirely to her taste, laidback Fitz had Mack's curiosity zinging like crazy.

Questions: Putting aside any small hope it had anything to do with her, was his mood business related? A family thing? While she'd seen the tenderness Fitz felt for Tom and his family, there was clearly tension between him and his father.

People had been talking at the party about what might happen when Fraser eventually retired—most saying Fitz was the natural successor, others not so sure he'd want the role. As always, she'd written down her notes that night, baulking for a mere moment upon deciding which file to put them in—the collaborative Future File or her Off the Record private file—before deciding on the former, as the staff knew who she was, and there had been no explicit instruction otherwise.

Not for this story, of course. Just information.

A couple of hours later, they arrived at The Rise. Like The Ridge, it offered small camps for group stays as well as privately situated accommodation. Instead of luxury cabins, the guests slept in large, romantic-looking Bedouin-style tents. Each came with bed, rug, floor cushions, solar power, mini ice box, and a short deck leading to a composting toilet and solar-heated treated-bore water shower—all laid out on platforms raised off the ground.

And while The Ridge had been perched on the edge of the magnificent gorge, there was still a sense that civilisation was within reach. Out here the isolation felt real.

While Fitz insisted on looking after the luggage, Mack and her Hideaway Haven backpack took a stroll to the communal kitchen and "living room," a large seated area hidden by trees, rocks, and shrubbery a hundred odd metres away from her tent.

Wooden furniture had been bolted to the concrete floor—no doubt to survive the storm winds—while a barbecue sat patiently in one corner. The tilted roof well overhead kept out the bright and heat of the sun, but did nothing to hamper the astonishing view.

Soft tufts of white cloud pottered across a cerulean blue sky. In the distance, a gargantuan curve of rust red escarpments rose in a sheer curtain of rock, and nearer, through a curving line of ghostly grey-green gum trees, came the shimmer of a great river.

Mack breathed in the fresh, rich, earthy air, and

marvelled that she had ever considered coming to this place penance.

She turned at the crack of a stick beneath a boot to find Fitz ambling her way, all big, and strong, and careful, the golden midday light running over him like a waterfall of sunshine.

"You good?" he asked.

"Admiring the view."

When she didn't look away, a smile hooked at the corner of his mouth.

"Happy to stay here while I set up my digs?" he asked.

"What are your 'digs'?"

"Camp set up off the side of the Land Rover."

"Sounds…comfy." She smiled innocently, not about to tell him that for a smidge there, she'd wondered if she'd found herself in a one-bed situation and hadn't been sorry about it.

Mack had found her way to the anniversary party the night before under the influence of a good head of steam at how things had been left between them, but beneath it had been a hollow ache at the thought of not seeing Fitz again.

Watching him squint thoughtfully out at the distance, eye crinkles crinkling, skin glistening in the high heat, the ache hadn't eased. If anything, it had morphed into a new kind of longing, something she'd only ever truly felt for concepts, for hopes and dreams, never for an individual, and certainly not one within reach.

Having lived with those other longings for a

really long time, the thought of taking a new one home with her did not sit well. So, as time was now ticking down till the day she left, she had to do what needed to be done to get it out of her system.

"Fitz?" she said, her pulse now beating hard behind her ears, as she readied to make the man a proposition—

"The others will be joining us soon," Fitz said, checking his heavy-duty watch, sunlight glinting off the pale hairs and the roping veins disappearing under the rolled-up sleeves of his shirt.

"The others?"

Mack heard voices as four men in heavy-duty hiking gear, with the iconic Hideaway Haven backpacks over their shoulders, came over the titular rise, a wilderness guide bringing up the rear with a large food cooler in hand.

"Lunch friends!" one of the guys called upon spying them. "Thank God. If I had to look at nothing but these mugs for another hour, I might have thrown myself in the river."

Mack looked at Fitz.

"Go," he said, his gaze roving over her face, even as he tilted his chin towards the chairs. "They're regulars. They're happy to answer any and all questions."

"Oh. Well, that's…really helpful. Thank you."

With a nod, he walked away, his cowboy hat low over his eyes. And something hard and hot twisted in the hollow space inside of her.

And yet, above and beyond any other needs

she might be feeling, she had a job to do. So, she brought up her Mackenzie-Lawler-on-the-job smile and got to work.

Evening falls softly over The Rise.

The streak of clouds to the west develops a quiet blush. Small groups of red-tailed black cockatoos wheel and squawk overhead, roosting in the taller eucalypts, the trunks now a soft pale pink. This clamour of colour is the language of dusk.

Mack looked up from her laptop to see if she'd come close to transcribing the savage beauty before her, only to rub exhaustion from her eyes.

Group after group had come by over the course of the afternoon, and while it had been beneficial for her story, she couldn't count the number of times she'd looked up from her spot hoping to see Fitz.

If this was a portent to how things might go when this was all over, she had to do something about it, and soon.

Then, as if she'd wished him just enough, he appeared.

Her heart skittered so happily as he neared, she sighed. *Oh help.* Was she so far down the rabbit hole she wasn't sure how to stop falling, *or* know how to scramble back out?

"All done?" she asked. "No more surprise guests?"

He nodded then took a seat by hers, sliding

down in the thing so he could put his feet up on another. "Human, at least."

Mack rolled her eyes, but curled her feet more tightly under her chair just in case.

Fitz glanced at her screen, then looked away.

"Want to see?" she asked, angling her laptop.

He closed his eyes, hands resting lightly on his flat belly. "Can't. Not till it's done. Your rules. Though I have no doubt it'll knock my socks off."

If Mack's heart had felt skittery before, after that it was in danger of leaping out of her chest. *She* knew she'd write something sensory, and engaging, and real, but the fact he believed it with such easy conviction had her wanting to climb over the table and ravage him then and there.

Huffing out a laugh, she said, "I wish I could record you saying that and show it to the guy who ambled up to me a week ago, all 'Get off my lawn.'"

Fitz opened one eye. "Was I that curmudgeonly?"

"One hundred percent," she said.

He harrumphed and closed his eyes again, and Mack kept to herself the fact that while on anyone else curmudgeonly might be a turn-off, on Fitz it was sexy as hell.

Knowing she'd not write another word now, Mack closed her laptop.

"Should I nudge you in a bit," she asked, "make sure you've not drifted off?"

"Maybe," he said after a few beats. "Been a while since I've had a daytime kip, but there's something about this spot, the different kind of quiet, that eases my blood."

Mack understood, at least a little, what he meant. Glancing at her laptop, she said, "I've been toying with how to describe it. While The Ridge requires some suspension of disbelief in order to feel truly immersed, out here it feels…infinite. And ancient. As if I can feel the hum of centuries past vibrating beneath my feet."

He blinked his eyes open, his dark gaze finding hers as he said, "That'll do it."

Heat hummed between them that had nothing to do with the baked earth beneath them.

"Question time?" she asked.

His mouth kicked up into a slow smile, which she took as a yes.

"If you could live any place in the world, would you still choose here?"

With a groan, Fitz dropped his feet to the floor and sat up, leaning forward, elbows on knees, so his hands were inches from her thighs.

"Is this for your piece, or…" Or did *she* want to know because it was starting to feel like she had skin in the game.

Mack shook her head. "Strike that."

"No. I'll answer it." Taking a moment to choose the right words, something she loved to watch him do, he said, "I have travelled. A lot. But no matter how far I roam there's a tug, right here…" He reached up and smacked his fist against his sternum, twice. "To come back." Then he asked, "You?"

She wondered if his motivation for asking was anything like her own.

"I travel a lot too," she said, "for *The Pulse*, but I'm in and out of a place before I see much more than the inside of a hotel, so I'm not sure I've ever really had the opportunity to find out if I love London the way that I do because I *love* it, or because its familiar."

She finished with a slight lift of a shoulder, as thoughts and feelings rocketed through her too quickly to get a hold of any of them.

While Fitz nodded, absorbing her words. Then pushed himself to standing. "It's getting dark. Time we head in."

"In" meaning Mack to her tent and Fitz to the far more basic set-up that had magically flipped out from the top of his Land Rover. When they came to a halt halfway between the two, Mack turned to face him.

With the glow of the soft golden solar lights inside her tent tracing the beautiful planes of his face, the column of his neck, the adorable misbend of his collar, she wasn't sure whether she wanted to say thank you, or good-night, or to ask if he ever had any time off and a hankering to see Big Ben.

"If you have a question," Fitz said, his voice like warm honey over gravel, "just ask it."

Only for what might be the first time in her

life, she had no questions in her head, just feelings. "Maybe…tell me something I'd never think to ask."

Fitz crossed his arms as he considered her request. Then his mouth flickered, as he looked off into the night. "Ask me my middle name."

"What's your—"

"Laurence. As in Laurie, from *Little Women*."

Well, that was sweet.

"Care to know how my brothers fared?" he asked, his voice dropping to an intimate drawl she felt in her very bones. "We have Jackson *Rochester*."

"Brilliant."

"Tom *Benedick*."

She clicked her fingers. "*Much Ado!*"

Fitz nodded. "Logan *Wentworth*."

"Love it."

"And Will's middle name was *Fraser*."

Mack's next breath felt trapped in her lungs. Will. Will as in Fitz's twin, who had died when he was terribly young. She schooled her expression and said, "Your father must have been so chuffed—"

"After Jamie Fraser. From the *Outlander* books."

"No!" she shot out, then at Fitz's slow nod, she laughed so hard she had to bend, hands on knees, when she felt a stitch coming on.

"And as my mother was reading *Pride and Prejudice* when pregnant with us, at which point she found out we were twins, she settled on Fitz and Will, almost immediately. Naming us after—"

"Fitzwilliam," Mack got out. "You're actually named after *Mr. Darcy*?"

Fitz nodded, the smile on his face honest and true. As if he was enjoying her reaction exactly as much as he'd expected he would. As if he knew her that well.

Mack stood, pinching her waist. "I think I'd have liked your mother very much."

"I know she'd have adored you."

Oh help, Mack thought and not for the first time when it came to this man. As moonlight, starlight, Fitz's inner light—whatever magic this man brought was all there in his gaze, right along with his intent.

"Are we off the record?" he asked, taking a step closer, till the toes of his boots kissed the toes of hers.

"If you wish."

"I wish it very much," he said, his hand landing on her waist, and waiting there. Then moving slowly around her back, before pausing. Giving her all the time in the world to let him know if she wasn't on board.

Only very much on board, the president of the fan club of on board, Mack curled her fingers in the front of his shirt.

"If I wasn't completely sure you were here for the reasons you say you're here," Fitz said, "I might honestly believe you were sent to torture me."

And with that he drew her to him and kissed her.

Despite the strength in the arm across her back, his kiss was achingly gentle, a quiet press of his lips to hers. Then a slightly deeper tasting. Testing how they fit, and learning what made her tremble.

Feeding the ache, Mack opened her mouth to him, and he did not hesitate. His tongue swept against hers, and it was wholly debilitating. Her knees went, her extremities lost all feeling as her blood pooled in the important places, and Fitz kissed and kissed and kissed her, slow, and wet, and solemn.

An age later, Mack slowly came to, breaths mingling as Fitz pressed his forehead to hers. Only to find she had one hand in his hair, the other gripping his backside, her leg curled proprietarily around his calf.

As she slowly extricated herself, limb by limb, Fitz lowered her to her heels, making sure she was steady before he let her go.

With a frown, he looked around to find his hat on the ground, where she must have knocked it. And when he stood, hat held over his heart, his hair was a glorious mess from her fierce hands.

"Go on then," he said, motioning with his chin for her to go inside.

She nodded, then stepped up into the tent.

He waited, outside, for her to zip the clear opening of the outer layer closed.

Then, slipping his hat onto his head, he was gone.

Leaving Mack in the opening, staring out into

the pitch-black night, wondering how she'd ever thought that kissing him again might make the hollow go away.

Now she felt as if there was a cavern inside of her that only he could fill.

CHAPTER TEN

THE NEXT MORNING, Mack woke with the birds, dressed, had breakfast in her tent, checked and repacked her backpack, then tried to write.

Only the heat was something fantastical; the humidity had to be nearing 100 percent. And every time she tried to write a word about the Haven she thought of Fitz, and the rumbling sounds he'd made as he kissed her the night before.

So instead, she messaged Priya with research questions. Answered a text from Annalise. Then, after a pause, she sent Crispin the first few paragraphs of what she'd written so far.

Within minutes he messaged her back.

CRISPIN: Going well?

It wasn't exactly effusive, but she was proud of herself, that the glimmer of joy at hearing from her brother refused to wane.

MACK: Going great! It's beautiful out here. You should come over for your next holiday.

Mack winced; the thought of her suit-and-tie brother coping with the flies and the sweat and lack of civilisation was laughable. Then again, she'd have said the same of herself a couple of weeks back, and look at her now, living in a tent as if it was nothing.

CRISPIN: Chomping at the bit to return, I imagine.

Mack glanced out at the shock of blue sky, and the gentle sway of the grey-green brush, and imagined Fitz lying back on his camp bunk by the four-wheel drive, one hand beneath his head, the other hand holding some book his mother had introduced to him.

Chomping wasn't the word she'd use.

MACK: Home next week!

CRISPIN: Come see me when you get back. We'll have lunch.

A minute later her paragraphs were returned to her with a half-dozen copy edits, and *Nice Work, CL* at the bottom.

While in the not-too-distant past she'd have taken that tiny token of approval like some might accept an Academy Award, this time she simply saw it as her due.

So, she put work aside for the day, dressed, applied sunscreen, grabbed her backpack, and zipped up her tent, only to round the corner right as Fitz was coming the other way.

"Morning!" she said breathlessly.

His eyes were hard, his jaw tight, his hair a glorious shag as if he'd raked his fingers through it all night long. It seemed Grumpy Fitz was back.

Meaning Mack's instinct was to go the other way. "It's such a beautiful day. I'm ready and raring to see what else is out here."

When Fitz's gaze flitted to hers and away again, Mack felt a flutter of apprehension. While in the past his determination to keep her at arm's length had been frustrating, this time, she knew it would hurt.

Then Fitz's phone buzzed in his pocket. When he ignored it, Mack said, "You can answer that if you want. I'm happy to wait."

When his gaze found hers, it was clear he wasn't daydreaming about last night as she was. There were hard things going on behind those steel-blue eyes, and she knew him enough to know no amount of questioning would shake them free.

So, she waited. An easy-going presence, with all the patience in the world, a guise she'd spent a lifetime perfecting.

After several long seconds, he cracked. "Bring togs?"

"I don't know what that—"

"Swimwear."

"Yes!"

"Get changed. We're going swimming."

* * *

Leaving the Land Rover when the terrain became too much, Mack followed Fitz over and through some pretty serious hiking territory.

The heat was something else, meaning her effort to get him out of his funk went by the wayside as she spent her energy swiping sweat from her eyes, not tripping over, and not asking why he wasn't answering the stream of messages buzzing at his phone.

"Are we there yet?" she asked.

A few feet in front of her, Fitz shook his head.

A minute later, "Are we there yet?"

There. A quick lift of the shoulders she was sure was a laugh.

She opened her mouth to ask again, only to hear a noise. "What's that sound?"

Fitz waited for her to catch up, then motioned for her to go first. A couple of minutes later, when she pushed back the brush, she saw they were at the summit of a sandstone cliff, looking down on a natural infinity pool.

"This is exquisite."

"It's not the most popular," Fitz said, moving alongside her, "or the biggest by any means, but it's my favourite on Kings Reach."

"I bet you say that to all the girls."

The look he gave her made it clear he did not. That she might even be the first he'd ever brought there, to his favourite place.

"Can we swim here?" she asked, her voice thin.

"We can. Or down there." He motioned to the edge where a waterfall cascaded into a shaded waterhole.

Mack's voice was tinged with awe as she said, "Which should we do?"

"Either. Both. The day is yours."

Whether he meant for her story, or just for her, she was not about to ask.

"I call…waterfall!" she said.

Fitz led the way.

By the time they made it down to the shaded waterhole below, if Mack didn't get in that water soon, she might literally expire.

Once Fitz gave the okay, she shucked off her hiking boots and socks, yanked off her top and shorts. Stepping from foot to foot, the rock scorching beneath her bare feet, she quickly reapplied sun cream, certain she could feel her skin screaming, then hurried to the water's edge.

"Take it slow," Fitz's voice called from his rock.

Mack, who already had a toe in the water, pulled back with a yelp. "Crocodiles?"

"Moss," he deadpanned.

Right. And yet she decided to wait. Just in case.

Looking back to see how he was coming along, Mack watched as Fitz tugged his shirt over his head in that way men did—from back to front in one smooth move. He scrunched it in a ball at his ridiculously sculptured chest, while he looked for somewhere to put it, then glanced up and found her watching.

Ogling more like, for the man was…*phwoar*. From the hugeness of his shoulders, to the strong outline of his pecs and the ridges of his six-pack, he was a study in masculine musculature built on fresh air, and good food, and hard work.

While she was a pasty, sunlight-deprived, indoor girl, scared of a little moss.

Panting a little—due to the heat!—she dragged her gaze back to his face to find him grinning. Which, to be fair, was an improvement on all the frowning she'd received so far that day.

Fitz blithely tossed the shirt to where his hat lay at a rakish angle over the branch of a bush, torso rippling as he twisted. Then he dropped his hands to his khakis, where he popped the button free, then slid the zip down, mesmerisingly, tooth by tooth. When his thumbs disappeared into his beltline and he began to whip his pants down, Mack blinked furiously and turned away.

Fitz's rough chuckle echoed off the sheer walls above.

Feeling his gaze on her, she took a slow step into the water, hissing slightly at the cool of it against her hot skin, then she adjusted her bikini bottoms, deliberately positioning them a good inch higher up her backside.

Fitz's litany of impressive curses gave her courage to amble deeper. When the water hit her knees, she stopped to acclimatise, only to hear water swishing behind her as he waded into the shallows.

He stopped a little deeper than she was, grabbed a handful of water and sluiced it over his hair. Mack watched in a stupor as the water ran in rivulets down his brown skin, catching on the hairs of his chest, cascading over his many muscles, and thought it a miracle the man was really real.

Then he flicked the excess from his hands, some caught her, and she squealed. He turned, a smile in his eyes. But it was quickly burned away as his gaze ate her up like dessert.

He slowly reached down to grab another handful of cool water.

"Don't you dare," she ordered.

"Then hurry up. The faster you get in, the sooner it feels great."

She waved a hand at him. "Look at you. You have way more meat on your bones than I do. And I am a warm bubble bath kind of girl—"

Fitz took three strides her way, slid an arm beneath her knees, another under her arms, then hoisted her against all that hot bare skin and carried her into the water.

Her backside hit the surface first, the sudden shock making her cry out. When he kept on walking, taking them deeper and deeper, she wrapped her arms around his neck, her legs about his hips, till she was full koala, sweat and sunscreen making it slippery business.

"You right there?" he asked.

Her gaze whipped from the water to his face to find it mere centimetres away. Tangled lashes, beautiful blue eyes. Rough stubble at his jaw. The line of his hat had left a light red mark across his forehead. Hers had no doubt done the same, but she did not care. She was too busy committing his face to memory, knowing she'd never in her life find its ilk again.

Then she unwrapped a hand from around his neck and ran her pointer finger over a scar cutting through the tip of his right eyebrow.

"Question. How did this happen?" she asked, as if that was her motivation for touching him rather than the fact that not touching him had become an impossible thing.

"Racing my brothers on horseback. Tree branch got me."

"And this?" she asked, the pad of her thumb running alongside a scar on the curve of his collarbone. His skin twitched under her touch.

"Fell off the barn landing after climbing up there trying to fetch a lost footy."

"Our barn?" she said, before she realised what that implied.

"Our barn," he concurred, his voice so deep she more felt than heard his words.

In fact, she felt so many things. The water lapping at her skin, the way the water bobbing her about had her centre rolling against the top of his boxer shorts, and the hardness therein.

She knew there were a million reasons to be careful, but in that moment, she could not think of a single one. She wanted to remember every single moment of this experience.

Fitz, feeling her tremble, must have thought her cold, as he wrapped his arms more fully around her and, shushing her protests, took them deeper into the water, only to make every sensation excruciatingly worse. In the best possible way.

"You can swim?" he asked, when the water lapped their necks.

"I can swim."

Gaze dropping to her mouth, he asked, "Do you *want* to swim?"

"What's the alternative?"

He glanced behind her to where the waterfall splashed into the pool several metres away.

Mack gasped as she took in the greenery tumbling down the craggy rock face, the waterfall a silken stream of white, curling over the red rock like translucent ribbons and turning the water a cloudy green as it filled with tiny bubbles.

She'd been so focussed on the man in her arms, she'd not realised they were in literal paradise.

"Come on," said Fitz, uncurling her from his body and making lazy strokes towards the fall.

Mack followed, the noise growing so loud it became impossible to hear one another, until they swam behind the curtain of water to where a small shaded grotto was filled with pretty mist.

There, away from prying eyes of wallabies and

corellas and whatever other creepy crawlies might come upon them, Mack didn't hesitate—she floated into Fitz's arms, curled her hand into his hair and kissed him.

Or maybe it was he who kissed her.

What did it matter when his arms wrapped around her, pulling her close as his mouth moved over hers with such surety, and need, and patent relief, and she quickly dissolved into blissful sensation and feeling.

She arched against his touch, as Fitz's calloused hands ran up and down her back, her head lolling as pleasure rolled through her. He took advantage, sliding kisses along her collarbone, whispering dirty promises against her skin that had her burning up and seeing red and filled with such want she had no words for any of it.

The man could not be accused of being subtle—not in looks, or skills, or mood. As a lover he was exactly as advertised: able, hungry, and extremely literate. So much so she didn't even feel the man undoing the string at her neck, until her bikini straps trailed over her décolletage. Then Fitz's mouth covered a bare nipple as he lathed it with his tongue.

When he moved to drag soft kisses between her breasts, Mack held his head in her hands, drawing it to her other breast. She felt him smile against her, as he licked a slow circle of her nipple, drawing out soft whimpers of agony and pleasure, before he took it into his mouth.

Needing more, wanting it all, Mack's hand ran

down his chest, scraping through the smattering of hair covering his pecs, before ducking beneath his boxer shorts to palm the huge hot length of him.

Fitz reared back, his hand dropping to cup hers.

Their eyes met—his dark, heavy-lidded, hers all but unseeing, she felt so wild with desire. When his fingers curled over hers, she stroked, down then up, revelling in the catch of breath in his throat, the pink rising into his cheeks, the throb of him in his hand.

Then, swearing beneath his breath, Fitz eased her hand away.

"Fitz," Mack begged, her voice laboured.

Over the roar of the waterfall he said, "I didn't bring you here for this."

"Yes, you did."

He lifted his eyes to hers and they were…serious. More than that, they were wretched. As if while she'd been giving herself over to the moment, he'd been beating himself up.

Swallowing hard, she lifted a hand to his cheek to run her thumb over the angle of his cheekbone, and slid another through a curl of his hair.

"Whatever is going on with you today, I understand why you might not want to talk to me about it."

And she did. Truly. But as she said the words, the hollowness inside her spread so deep and so wide, she had no choice but to add, "But you need to know that this, you and me, is not something you need to apologise for. Ever. Rushed as this might feel, I'm right here with you."

Fitz looked into her as if he was able to read her, heart and soul. Then, delving his hands into her hair, he pulled her in for a long, sweet, lingering kiss. The kind that spoke of tenderness, and trust. The kind she feared might never be bettered as long as she lived.

When he pulled back, breathing heavily, for his sake as much as her own she said, "I'm famished. Could we find somewhere to have lunch?"

"First, let me…" Gaze trailing up her body, he gently gathered the strings of her bikini top, slowly brought them back up her chest, pads of his thumbs catching on the hard peaks of her nipples as he smoothed the triangles back into place.

How Mack managed not to tear the thing off and beg him to have his way with her then and there she could not say. Some inner strength had her gathering her hair at her nape, making space for his deft fingers to tie the string back into a bow, after which he pressed a kiss to the spot where her neck met her shoulder.

Then, taking her hands and pulling them around his neck, he turned her so she was lying against his back and swam them back out of their fairy tale cave, around the darling waterfall, into the cool of the pool so they could collect their things and leave this place behind.

After they returned to camp, Mack begged the need for time to write.

Fitz knew she was gifting him the afternoon to

sort himself out, meaning he'd done a rubbish job of hiding the fact he needed it.

Still, it took him till evening, sitting by the fire he'd lit in the pit not far from their spot, watching the flames rise and settle, to deal with the messages that had been coming at him all day.

Ned and Julian had sent a photo of the bottle of red they were sharing on his behalf. Friends he'd met on travels, friends from school days, locals he'd known for forever had all sent texts.

He saved the brothers' group chat—now entitled All the Kings Men—for last.

LOGAN: Happy birthday, mate, Hope it's a good one.

TOM: Dammit. I wanted to be first. Happy birthday, little bro.

LOGAN: Little? Did you not notice the size of the guy these days?

TOM: You do not understand the struggle of being older than you both while being shorter than one and bench-pressable by the other.

Looking at the time stamps, they'd gone back and forth for a good half an hour without needing Fitz to be a part of it. In the past he'd have felt left out; now he understood absurdity was their way of sending care on a day when he needed it most.

Prepping to shoot back his thanks, his phone pinged.

JACKSON: Thinking of you.

Then…

JACKSON: Both.

Fitz's eyes went from fireside dry to prickly as hell in half a second. He swore beneath his breath and looked up, watching the flickers of firelit ash waft into the clear star-speckled sky till the feeling passed.

"Fitz?" Mack's voice came to him on the evening breeze.

Fitz placed his phone face-down on the bench seat, stood, and ran his hands down the sides of his jeans before turning to find her strolling his way.

Mack's hair was down, wavy from the swim. She wore a floaty green dress that fell from thin straps at her shoulders to swish about her ankles, and with the fire dancing over her skin she looked ethereal. And heartbreakingly lovely.

Doubling down on the goddess thing, she had a bottle of light beer in each hand and passed one his way. "Thought you could do with one of these."

"Contraband," he chastised, taking it gratefully, the condensation making it slip from her fingers into his.

"I saw it wasn't on the menu out here," she said,

hitching a shoulder. "Figured I'd stash a couple in case I was afraid of the dark."

"How you doing so far?"

She looked up. "I've never seen so many stars."

Fitz held the heel of his palm against the bottle top, and knocked it against the bench so the cap sprang free. Then he held out a hand in offer to open hers, but she leaned towards his bench and opened hers with a deftness that had him growling, "Marry me. Right now."

Mack laughed, bringing the drink to her lips and taking a long swig as she took a seat next to him.

"Where did you learn to do that?" he asked, his voice gruff.

"Oxford."

"Ah."

A log shifted, snapped, and fell into the fire, and they both turned to watch the smatter of sparks.

Then his phone buzzed, and buzzed, and buzzed again, and he imagined Tom perking up with a *Excuse me, strange man, this is a private chat between brothers* or some such dig at Jack. When his phone went quiet, he figured the oldest King brother had gone dark once more.

"Hungry?" Fitz asked.

Mack shook her head. Then, as if she figured she'd given him quite enough time to brood, she looked his way. "Your phone has been insistent today."

Fitz twirled the bottle between his fingers. "It's my birthday."

"Oh! Well, happy birthday," she said, holding out her beer.

He clinked the bottom of her bottle with his, and they each took a small swig, gazes tangling. Which is why he saw the moment it hit her.

"If it's your birthday, then…then its Will's birthday too. Oh, Fitz. I feel like such a gulumph, trying to glitter you out of your funk this morning." Then, "Unless you'd like to talk about it? About him? Off the record, of course."

Fitz noted the anguish in her expression at having to clarify. He wondered if everyone in her life thought twice before sharing themselves, knowing how dedicated she was to her work. How isolating that must be, far more than distance could be.

While talking about Will wasn't something he did, with anyone—for there had been so much talk, so much blame, so much anger for such a long time after it had happened, he'd closed up that part of himself in order to survive it.

Only not talking hadn't helped ease his pain. Looking into Mack's pretty hazel eyes, Fitz made a choice.

Putting his beer on the ground at the side of his boot, Fitz watched the fire as he said, "We were a high-risk pregnancy, Will and I. We had something called twin-to-twin transfusion syndrome, which pretty much means that I took too much blood, he not enough. Treatment, before and after we were born, saved me from heart failure and kept him alive. But even so, he was born really small, while I was, well…"

Fitz held out his arms—a big guy, healthy as a horse, despite all he'd put his body through in his early twenties.

"Are you okay?" Mack asked. "Now?"

"Physically? I'm fine. Transfusions, blood thinners, doctor magic sorted me out quick smart. Though my mother insisted it meant my heart had to be bigger than normal, to hold all that extra weight."

Mack gave him a soft smile, and once again it hit how much his mum would have adored her.

"But Will…" Fitz said. "He was never like the rest of us."

"How so?" Mack asked.

"He was quiet, shy, never much into the roughhousing that was our family love language. He was also wildly creative." Fitz didn't realise he'd sat taller till he couldn't reach his drink without bending. "Loved to draw, loved music. The guitar in the library?"

Mack nodded.

"He'd only just started teaching himself when… He loved the barn cats. All feral, every one given a name. But the farming side of things he could take or leave."

All of it Fitz's fault. Taking from him, with a King's hunger to survive, before Will even took a breath.

Memories piling in now, Fitz's voice felt far

away as he said, "It had been terrible dry that year, stressful, lots of dead cattle. When Dad called for us to all help on a hay drop, I took Will aside, told him not to ask to stay home as he usually did. And if…if Dad got frustrated, the way he did sometimes when Will didn't rise to physical challenges, not to recoil, to take it."

Fitz rubbed hard fingers over his temples as he remembered the tension coiled inside him as he'd given Will the barrage of panicked instructions. The earnestness in Will's face as he'd listened.

"It's fuzzy now, but something had happened on the hay run—Tom made a joke, Dad bit back, and Will… Will did what I told him to do and ended up banished to the back of the ute."

Fitz swallowed as the final part of the memory grew clearer. The searing heat, the incessant dry, the scent of petrol in his nose. "It can't have been a minute later when the truck hit a wombat hole. One second Will was there, the next he was gone. Fallen off the back."

Jack cradling Will on the ground. Tom and Logan yelling. His father's face white as a ghost. After that it turned cloudy again.

"It's been rough, over the years, watching the others blame Dad. But… I don't know. We were all strung out, making bad choices under difficult circumstances."

"It was an accident," Mack said. "You were a little kid. And it was a terrible, tragic *accident*."

When he glanced at Mack, she was swiping

tears from her cheek. Then she leaned towards him and curled her fingers around his. They sat that way, saying nothing for a good long while. Till, like logs on the fire, transforming from wood to ash, things inside him shifted. Resettled. Quieted.

"Thank you for telling me," Mack said.

"Now you see why my birthday isn't my favourite day of the year." He looked at her through one eye. "Apologies if you had to bear the brunt of it earlier."

She lifted a shoulder in a half shrug. "I'm just mortified I've not got you a gift."

Fitz huffed out a laugh, surprised as hell to know he could.

Then, looking around as if one might suddenly present itself, Mack asked, "Is there cake? Do you want me to sing?"

"I want you to do whatever makes you happy."

Her gaze shot back to his, pupils dark, eyes bright in the firelight. "Are you hungry? Do you want me to put something together from the ice box?"

Fitz reached behind him for the small esky and pulled out sausages, white bread, and tomato sauce.

"Gourmet," she cooed.

"Will's favourite."

"Perfect."

"That's not the half of it," he said, then pulled out a bag of—

"Marshmallows!" At that she clapped, then

looked to the fire. "I've literally never roasted marshmallows over a fire before. Chestnuts, yes, during picture-postcard Lawler Christmases. Awful things. Taste like bark. I can't believe how ridiculously excited I am."

Fitz could. For Mack was a determined seeker of joy, a noticer of wonder. Add her astuteness, her brazen ambition, her willingness to give things a red-hot go, her desire to do right, and the way she kissed as if it was her last day on earth and she had no time to be coy—he'd never met anyone like her.

He'd spent a lifetime determined that when Will had gone, he'd taken all of Fitz's softer feelings with him. Then Mack Lawler had come along, and now he was feeling all the things, joy, apprehension, regret, longing, hope.

He could only hope it would be worth it.

"How a person roasts marshmallows says a lot about them," Fitz cited, watching Mack's blackened marshmallow holding on to the end of her stick by nothing short of a miracle.

Pulling it from the fire, she gave him a quick look. "That so?

"You like to see how far you can push things."

She curled her tongue towards her crispy treat and pulled back when it was still too hot. "And there I was thinking crispy on the outside and gooey on the inside just tasted better. What does your way say about you?"

Fitz stuck a marshmallow on the end of his stick,

rolled it over a glowing log, then slid it back out again. "I don't muck about. In, out, done." He clamped his teeth over the edge and tugged it free.

Over the top of hers, lips still pursed, Mack watched, eyes darkening. Till her marshmallow fell off the end of her stick and landed in the dirt with a sticky *thwap.* "What? No! I was so close."

Fitz, feeling the effects of the overtones of their conversation, cleared his throat and handed her the bag so she could get another.

"I think I overdid it anyway," she said, shoulders slumped. "Too much of a good thing."

"Life's short," he said, voice low. "Indulge."

Her gaze shot back to his. Their earlier conversation, all that had happened to Will, hovering between them.

Then Mack yawned a most impressive yawn.

Fitz laughed. "Why don't you head to bed. I'll clean up here."

"Not happening, birthday boy."

Mack packed up the food and rubbish, while Fitz dampened the fire, kicking at the embers with his boots and covering it with dirt till every lick of a spark was gone.

The glow from Mack's tent led them back towards their accommodations. Once there, Mack stepped up onto the platform, bringing her to near eye level.

"Happy birthday, Fitz."

"Thank you," he said. "And thank you for making it…not terrible."

She smiled, moonlight kissing her cheeks, her collarbone, her mouth, a slick of molten marshmallow stuck to the edge of her bottom lip.

"You have leftovers."

Mack swiped her tongue over her lips but missed.

"May I?"

Fitz stepped closer, cupping her chin, the feel of her soft skin under his touch sending shards of heat to his centre. Tugging his thumb over the spot, it didn't budge. Then, knowing it was the only answer, he leaned in and pressed his lips to hers. They were soft, and sweet, and willing. And as he pulled away, he let his tongue sweep over the hint of marshmallow, till it was all gone.

When he made to let go, Mack grasped his wrist. "Don't," she said. "Don't go."

"If the dark does get you, I'll be just around the corner."

She shook her head, sliding her hand down his arm till her fingers entwined with his, then, twisting his arm behind her back, she said, "Every birthday boy needs a present."

Then she leaned all the way in and kissed him.

CHAPTER ELEVEN

MACK GASPED AGAINST Fitz's mouth, as his hands moved to her backside, pulling her to him, so she had no doubt he was very much with the program.

Then he lifted her and backed her into the tent, letting her go only to pull down the tent's zip. "Mozzies," he explained.

Swaying on unsteady legs, Mack said, "I don't care if the entire Australian coat of arms is on its way. Get back here."

Grinning, Fitz went to her, buried his face in her neck, nuzzling her earlobes, licking into her mouth, telling her in detail how much he loved the taste of her skin. When the backs of her knees hit the bed, she fell back, arms outstretched bouncing once, blinking up at the twinklers lining the seams of her tent.

Lifting up onto her elbows, she looked across the room to find Fitz at the end of the bed. His hair had fallen over his forehead, his jaw was tight, and his eyes were so dark there was not a lick of blue to be seen. His big chest rose and fell, his hands clenched and unclenched as his sides. The fact that she could bring a man like him to a state like this might be one of the great highlights of her life.

Shuffling up onto her knees, she moved to the end of the bed, crooked a finger till he came to her. Reaching up, she swept the hair from his face. He swallowed, hard, when her thumb ran over the bump of his Adam's apple. Harder again when her hand moved down his chest, over his belt buckle, to cup the hard bulge in his khakis.

With a growl, he climbed onto the bed. Laughing, she attempted to shuffle back on her knees, before falling back again as he moved over her. Then his mouth was on hers, taking her under with deep, lush kisses that had her writhing with the need to have him. All of him.

But then he was gone, leaving her alone on the bed, dress askew, lips puffy, panting.

"Hitch," he demanded, curling her dress up to over her thighs. She lifted and shifted till he pulled the maxi dress over her head, leaving her in nothing but her favoured plain white cotton underpants.

When his touch wasn't on her, alleviating the thrills scooting over her skin, once more she lifted onto her elbows this time to find Fitz taking off his shirt, muscles bulging as he whipped the thing down his arms, and, *oh my heavenly stars*, the man was something else.

Meaning it took her a second to realise he was folding his shirt and placing it on the chair in the corner of the tight space. Then did the same with his khakis.

This beast of a man, all hard muscle, and scars, and stories that required great finesse and patience to untangle, read books his mum loved, stacked the dishwasher, and folded his clothes. If she wasn't already halfway to love-struck, that tipped her right over the edge.

The serious bulge in his boxer shorts didn't hurt either. When he reached down and adjusted himself, it was a miracle Mack didn't come apart then and there.

Reaching for his khakis again, he pulled out an old-fashioned leather wallet, slid a condom free, and held it gently between his teeth, then tossed his pants with a little less care back onto the chair.

Tossing the condom onto the spare pillow, he climbed onto the bed and lay down beside her, and went right back to kissing her for all he was worth.

Mack wrapped her leg about his and let her hands rove all over, touching all the places she'd ached to touch for days. Months, if she included the time spent scrolling through photos of the man for "research purposes."

And when Fitz's calloused hand ran over her breast, then down her side and into her underwear, delving into her slick centre in one swift move, she bucked off the bed, mouth open on a gasp that he captured with his mouth.

Giving her no respite, he teased, and traced, and caressed, and ground with the heel of his palm, following her whimpers and whispers of *yes*, not abating even when her fingers bit into his back, mouth open against his meaty shoulder to stifle her scream as wave after wave of intense pleasure rolled through her.

And there Fitz kept her, slowing, easing, but not stopping, holding her on the edge with the gentlest of touches. Pleasure rippled through her till she could no longer stand it, then, after tipping over the edge once more, she collapsed to the bed. Needing air, and light, and the cool of the sheets to remind her she was earthbound.

When she eventually had the wherewithal to open her eyes, he was on his side, one leg trapping hers, his gaze roving over her heat flushed body as his fingers traced their way over her oversensitised skin, muscles fluttering at his touch. And when he leaned down to kiss her breast, right over her heart, Mack felt a sob tighten the back of her throat.

She tried to tell herself that her feelings for the guy were potent attraction born of forced proximity. But with the slightest shift of perspective that became intimacy of two people spending copious amounts of time together, and actually getting to know one another. Which was something she'd not experienced on the job, or in life, not in this way, not ever.

And in that moment, she knew she was one who'd been given a gift.

"Fitz," she whispered.

His gaze lifted to hers. "Tell me what you want and it's yours."

"You," she said, so many emotions rolling through her, the final one a kick of sorrow that this had to end. Hand roving down his arm, over his hip, beneath the waistband of his underwear, she said, "Now."

The moment she gave the word, his shorts were gone. Her underpants went next. She laughed, joy filling her as he flung both across the room.

When he kneeled over her, his gaze solemn, eyes danger dark, she took him by the chin and waited for his eyes to find hers. "Promise me I'm not taking advantage. It being your birthday, and an emotional time, and all."

"I give you full permission to take advantage of me as often as you like," he said, taking her hand from his jaw, sliding her thumb into his mouth, and biting down gently till she yelped.

Then, taking both hands in one of his, he held them over her head as he kissed her, deeply, his tongue sweeping into her mouth. Then glancing up, instructing her to keep her hands there, his clever fingers moved between her legs once more, sending her into orbits of pleasure.

And when her legs fell open of their own volition, he moved over her, nudged her centre once, twice, then entered her in one long, hot swoop.

She dragged in a gasping breath, her hands whipping to grasp his back. Pleasure building, building, again, as he rocked into her. The broad muscles of his back clutching under her grip, the planes of his magnificent backside clenching beneath her heels as she wrapped her legs around him, angling him deeper, sweeter.

For all that the man was not a talker in life, he whispered terms so dear and hot and mind-blowingly sexy against her neck till she cried out with each thrust. And while she could feel how close he was, he waited for her to hurtle over the edge before following her, and into oblivion they went.

"So that happened," Mack murmured as she lay curled up against Fitz, fingers playing with the hairs on his chest.

"About time, I'd say."

"Hear, hear." Her voice became sleepier by the second.

And while he felt sated to the tips of his toes, his mind ticked over with more questions than he could possibly field.

While this woman had burst into his life and turned it inside out, what if, for her, everything had been leading up to this, and now it was done? Did it even matter, when she was about to go back to her life, letting him finally go back to his? The world was not as small as a lot of people out this way thought it was; could they find a way to see one another again after her stint was done?

Or should he stop overthinking and start digging the moat and rebuilding his old defensive wall right now?

Then Mack, so close to sleep her breaths were

evening out, her fingers now resting gently against his chest, said, "I don't want this to end."

"This?" he asked, running a hand over her hair and down her back, hardening, again, as she rolled into his touch.

"You and me. Fighting and making love. We're not even together, and you're still the best boyfriend I've ever had by a country mile." With that she let out a soft sigh and fell asleep.

Fitz stared at the tented ceiling for over an hour. Then, uncurling himself from under her trusting grip, he slipped back into his clothes, took one last look at Mack, dark hair splashed across her pillow, worn out by fresh air and sunshine. And him.

When his chest squeezed, painfully, he headed out into the night.

The air was cool on his skin, the stars an absolute riot. After washing up quickly at the outdoor tap, he lay down on the small cot under the canopy beside the Land Rover. Sleep nowhere near ready to take him, he pulled out his phone.

Whereas earlier that day checking his messages had brought him out in a sweat, now his head was clear. And so, he texted back.

FITZ: Better late then never.

Tom instantly messaged back.

TOM: Bea and I rang the house hours ago, thank you very much. Only you weren't there.

She wanted to sing you a song she "wrote." It's happy birthday but she changed out your name to Captain Poopy Pants.

FITZ: Sorry I missed it.

TOM: How you doing?

FITZ: Alright, actually.

FITZ: Bea up?

TOM: Sheesh. I hope not.

Fitz looked at his watch to find it was officially the next day.

FITZ: Thank you, all of you, for the birthday messages. I appreciate it.

FITZ: I know Will would have too.

TOM: [heart emoji]

TOM: Heard from Dad at all?

Fitz paused before tapping:

FITZ: Not today.

Fitz watched the three dots and could *feel* Tom thinking. No doubt blaming the old man still. He had to hope Charlie, and her good sense, would knock that out of him in good time.

TOM: Well, here's to Will. Sweet kid, much missed. Definitely would have come up with far more creative names for this chat than I ever have.

FITZ: Not a doubt.

FITZ: Night Tom.

TOM: Night little bro.

Smiling, Fitz put his phone on charge, put his arm under his head, closed his eyes, and went to sleep.

Mack woke to the sound of the outdoor shower pumping outside her tent.

And while it usually took her a few seconds to remember where she slept, the tangle of sheets around her naked body and the ache in muscles she'd not used in years brought it all back to her in a second.

And now he was out there, naked. She pictured water sliding from his hair, over his beefy shoulder, the muscles of his back, into the dip above his backside.

The water turned off, and her eyes fluttered open, and she slowly slid her hand out from between her legs.

"Time to rise and shine, for it is a new day," she told herself as she rolled out of bed, wrapping the sheet around herself as she unzipped her tent and padded outside. Right as Fitz came walking by, jeans unbuttoned and low on his hips, naked from the waist up, running a small towel over his hair.

"Hey," he said, "did I wake you?"

She shook her head. "Maybe. That's okay."

When his face creased into an indulgent smile, taking in her sheet robe and her mussed hair, she pulled a face and said, "This is morning me."

Fitz breathed out slowly, then stepped onto the platform, pulled her into his arms, and kissed her. "Good morning, morning you." Then, "Now, I have to head off for a couple of hours. Will you be alright here?"

"Where are you going?"

"Something's not right with the North B2 bore windmill. I'm closest."

Catching three quarters of that at most, Mack said, "You mean *we're* closest."

Fitz spared her a glance.

Mack didn't like its implication. Especially when she'd woken in the middle of the night, found him missing from her bed, and begun to hyperventilate at the thought of doing so for the rest of her life.

The only way she'd been able to get back to sleep was running scenarios in her mind.

Questions: How much leave did she have banked? How far in advance did she have to apply for time off? If she came back, not as a customer but as…a friend of the family, could she actually contribute? Or would she, as seemed to be her lot in life, simply get underfoot?

"Listen up, buddy," she said, digging in. "You might like to picture me sitting at some neat little desk, tapping out my stories in temperature-controlled ease."

Gosh, that actually sounded really nice. And for the first time since she'd arrived, she felt a little homesick for her sweet home office on the third floor of her terraced house, with its view over the cottage garden her neighbours kept just so.

"But I can lift things," she said, regaining her train of thought. "Hold things. Do hard things."

Fitz's mouth curved into a slow smile. "First up, I'm aware of how adept you are at doing hard things."

A flush rushed into Mack's cheeks.

"Secondly, when I picture you, you're not sitting at a desk. Though now you've put the image there, I can work with it."

Ignoring his serious flirting game, and the acres of masculine chest, and the fact that the top button of his jeans was already undone, Mack said, "Let me help. Not for the story. For me."

"Fine," he said, jumping off the platform and heading to his car. "We leave in five."

"What do I need?" she called, madly uncurling herself from the confines of her sheet. "My backpack?"

Fitz waved over his shoulder and said, "I've got you."

And Mack never wished so hard for something to be true.

Mack and Fitz stood, hands on hips, squinting up at a classic-looking windmill, its blades tipping listlessly this way and that while a handful of cattle crowded the trough below.

"What do you think is wrong, exactly?" Mack asked.

"Tail vane's been damaged. Without it, no power, no water, stressed cattle. No telling when they've last had a drink."

The cattle were huge, now she was up close. Mack rifled through Sinclair's advice regarding crocodiles and spiders but couldn't remember hearing how to handle cattle, so figured she'd follow Fitz's lead.

"Do you know how to fix it?" she asked, as Fitz took a ladder off the rack atop the car.

"Patch job," said Fitz, pulling down rope and a toolbox. "Till the mechanics can get out here to fix it."

Mack nodded, then swiped a hand over her forehead.

Noticing, Fitz said, "If you stay with the car, keep the windows open and fluids up."

Mack squared her shoulders. "I'm here to help."

His gaze held hers for a long second, then he nodded and said, "Come on then."

Mack took a few gulps before slinging the water skin over her shoulder. Then, grabbing the rope and slinging it over the other, she did her best not to topple under the weight.

Fitz wouldn't worry if things might be beyond his capabilities, he'd just get the job done. And in that, at least, they were the same. On that flicker of positivity, she metaphorically rolled up her sleeves and followed.

Two hours later, shoulders in agony, a blister on her right hand, scratched and bruised all over, Mack watched as, with a grudging creak, the windmill began to turn.

And while the urge to whoop and punch the air was there, she was utterly spent. When Fitz looped the rope over his own shoulder so she didn't have to carry it, she was so grateful.

At the car, she waited, like a lump, for Fitz to load up. Then, with the boot still open, he crooked a finger her way, and said, "Sit."

She trudged to the back of the car and did as she was told.

"Let's clean this up," he said, thumb running along the edge of a particularly nasty looking scratch on her forearm.

The first swipe of antiseptic was cold and sharp. She bit her lip to stop from crying out. Fitz gentled his touch all the same.

"When did you last have a tetanus shot?" he asked.

"Just before I came. They made me. They made me come here. They made me get stabbed with a needle. And they're never going to give me a promotion. They just want me out of the way—"

Fitz tipped her chin so she looked at him. "Take a breath. That's right. And another. Why do I get the feeling there's more going on here than a cut arm?"

Mack, mortified, and probably suffering from heat-stroke, and not nearly as able to lift heavy things as she'd hoped she might be, dropped her face into her hands and hid in the darkness for a few long moments till she could collect herself.

"How do you work that hard," she asked, "day in, day out?"

"Why?" Fitz asked, his tone mild. "Are you looking for a change of career?"

She sobbed out a laugh. Then sniffed and wiped a quick finger under her nose. "I just hoped I might be of more use out there today."

"What is going on in that labyrinthine mind of yours?"

"Many, many things. At all times."

Fitz's smile was quiet, and thoughtful, and if he kept looking at her that way she might burst into tears.

Mack was not a crier, but it was as if everything she'd been through over the past few months hit her at once—the lack of faith, the banging her head against a professional wall, the fact Crispin still didn't see her as anything but a late-onset little sister. Maybe this swell of rage, and longing, and disappointment was years in the coming.

And poor Fitz was simply in the wrong place at the wrong time.

He scratched at the back of his neck. "My father told me something the other day, and I didn't think much of it, but now I wonder… Let me get this right. He said it was your brother's idea that you come here. That he thought your wheels were spinning back home and you needed a challenge. Something to get your teeth stuck into."

Mack sniffed again. "Crispin said that?"

"Apparently so."

If this was true, if third-hand information hadn't been twisted somehow, it meant that Crispin hadn't sent her away as punishment. He'd sent her away because he saw her potential. Because he was giving her a serious chance to write the story of her life.

"I have to go home soon," she said, lifting her gaze to Fitz.

"I know."

"I want to. I miss it. I miss the cold. And curry. And shooing away the naughty squirrel who is obsessed with my hazelnut tree. But…"

Fitz slid his hand into her hair, his thumb tracing her cheek, swiping away a single tear. And when he said, "I know," again, she knew that what he was really saying was that *he knew*. He knew that while she wanted to go home, a big part of her wanted to stay, with him.

And in that moment Mack's heart up and left her chest and gave itself over to Fitz King.

A beat later, she tried to haul it back. But when he lifted her arm so he could place a kiss upon the bandage, she knew it was too late.

"I wasn't completely useless out there, was I?"

"Not even slightly," he said, as he packed up the first aid kit.

"If I bought one of those Akubra hats you all love so much, you'd soon forget I wasn't born here."

It was a joke, clearly, but Fitz's lack of affirmation still made her heart clutch. She went to slide from the boot, only Fitz's hands landed on her hips, staying her there.

His eyes were serious as he said, "I like that you weren't born around here. I like that your sensibilities are broader than all this. I like that you have opinions, and aren't afraid to voice them. I like that you refuse to be daunted by the notion of doing hard things, even if they are wildly outside of your comfort zone. I like you…"

She waited for the rest of his sentence, then realised that was it.

Fitz *liked* her. But not only that, he liked her for the very reasons others had chastised her—for being unmanageable, overambitious. He liked her for the things she liked most about herself.

Mack reached for him, pulling him into the gap between her knees. And while the emotions rising inside her were fierce, she no longer felt a need to cry.

Fitz's dark gaze roved over her face. Then he pressed his mouth to one cheek, then the other. His lips were hot, the stroke of his hand sure as it slid deeper into her hair, goose bumps trailing in the wake of his touch like glitter along her veins.

"Why must you use words such as labyrinthine?" she said, curling her leg around his.

"Did I use it wrong?" he asked, kissing his way down her neck.

"You used it perfectly. Which only makes me like you too."

He pulled back to look into her eyes. Then, with a growl, he pressed her back onto the floor of the boot, her laughter joining the bustle of the warm breeze and the creak of the distant windmill as the soundtrack to their kiss.

The next day they did nothing, and went nowhere.

Fitz read a copy of *The Thorn Birds* he found in the glove compartment, while Mack worked on her article. That was in between showering together, napping together, sitting in the living room watching the sun set together.

Fitz couldn't remember a single day of his life when he wasn't doing, moving, keeping his mind busy so it didn't spiral. Only that day, the thoughts gathering in the back of his mind felt intentional, as if all the strings of his life were twisting together.

Mack, leaving.

Kings Reach, in jeopardy.

The Haven, caught in the middle.

Sitting on the firepit bench, facing the tent where Mack sat cross-legged in bed tapping away at her laptop, Fitz pulled out his phone and called Logan.

"Brother," Logan said as hello. "Did you read the latest legal brief—"

"Stop," Fitz said, and not softly. "This isn't about the trust. Not directly. This is about Hideaway Haven, the lease, ownership, management—I want to shake things up."

"Now?" Logan asked. "The deal you have gives you the most flexibility possible. This is not the time to mess with it."

"See, now, I disagree." *Big swings*, he thought, feeling the knot inside him begin to unravel as he explained his plan. A plan not to make it easy to extricate the Haven from the Reach, but to make it nearly impossible.

His father had said to figure it out. And while it was a risk, proving to his father how much Kings Reach meant to him felt like the only piece of the puzzle he could control.

"Will you do it?" Fitz asked.

"Will Dad even consider it?" Logan asked, though Fitz could hear him typing already.

Fitz thought back on breakfast the other day, the glint in his father's eye when he'd said how shrewd he'd always thought Fitz to be.

"I'd bet the farm."

"Let's hope it doesn't come to that."

When Mack's phone beeped several times, she flinched. For she'd been deep into her article, putting what might be the final shine on what she was sure was the best thing she had ever written.

Untangling her feet from the messed-up sheets, she tugged her phone from the charger and sat on the edge of the bed. Only to find a slew of messages that had come through at once.

PRIYA: (voice message) Mack Attack! Place is buzzing. Your brother just showed his face here. Spent half an hour chatting with Alicia.

ALICIA: Darling! You've been given a reprieve. Next flight you can, come on home.

FROM THE DESK OF CRISPIN LAWLER: Appointment, Lunch: 12:30 p.m., 29 October. All parties to confirm ASAP.

PRIYA: (voice message) I heard you're on your way back. Huzzah! Cocktails the moment you arrive.

"Everything okay?"

Mack blinked at the sight of Fitz standing in the entrance to her tent, one hand in his jeans' pocket, the other holding his hat to his chest.

Fitz glanced at the phone she was white-knuckling in her lap.

"Yes. Yes! Fine. Great." *Except.* "I've just heard word that I've been called back early. I guess they've loved the pages I sent and think I have enough, so…"

She looked up as a shadow flickered over his face.

"When do you need to go?"

She opened her mouth and closed it, unable to say the words *As soon as possible.* For Fitz's scent was still on her, her skin covered in invisible tattoos in the places he had touched her.

He stepped inside, tossed his hat to the chair, and paced, slowly. "It'll take half an hour to pack up. We could have you at the homestead within three hours."

"Fitz," she said, sliding off the bed, her words thick, her view watery. "You know I'm not ready to…to leave."

You. She should have said *I'm not ready to leave you.* But the word stuck in her throat. Despite all the reasons he'd given her to trust that this wasn't some everyday thing for him either, she *couldn't* trust that when it came to the crunch, he'd choose her.

How could he, when his life was here?

Why would he, when those who *should* have never had?

Only some flicker of fight, some piece of her wasn't ready to give up. Walking up to him, she said, "You know what would be a great end to the story?"

Jaw tight, gaze grave, he said, "What's that?"

"Come with me!"

A single eyebrow shot north. "To London."

"Yes!" she said, the idea gaining merit the more she thought about it.

"To what end?" he asked, voice deepening, hand cupping her elbow, roving up her arm, as if even now, as things grew fraught, he couldn't help but touch her.

All of which meant it took her a minute longer than it ought to realise he'd not said *No.*

"It could be…" What was that movie? "A *Crocodile Dundee* thing. Outback guy in the big city, interacting with the kinds of people who would find themselves changed by having experienced all this."

She waved a hand towards the outdoors. When she turned back to him, he'd moved closer.

Then, voice cracking, just a smidge, she added, "People like me."

"Mack," he said, his voice subterranean, his hand now roving down her back.

Refusing to stop herself this time, she slid her arms around his waist and leaned her head against his chest. "You've been so generous, showing me what you love so much about your home. Come with me, let me show you all that's great about mine."

After what felt like an interminable amount of

time, Fitz said, "I do have a brother in London. Jackson, infamously private hotelier. You might have heard of him?"

"Maybe?" she said. Wild to think Jackson King had once loomed so large in her vision, now the man was irrelevant to her, bar how he figured in Fitz's response.

Which was: "It's high time I paid him a visit."

"You'll come?" she asked, pulling back so she could see his face.

"I'll come."

With a wholly uncool squeal, Mack threw herself into his arms.

Already plotting ways she could make the man see why London was such a part of her, but also that this thing between them might actually be big enough, special enough, to span continents.

CHAPTER TWELVE

MACK'S KNEE JIGGLED like crazy as together they took a black cab from Heathrow to the city, while Fitz chatted to the cabbie and showed her photos he'd sent Tom to show little Bea.

Her discomposure wasn't helped by the fact that, in a gorgeous navy pea coat over a cream Henley tee and beige chinos, bar the glorious tan, the man looked like he'd lived in London his whole life.

Shaking off the niggle that brought on, Mack narrowed her focus on what was ahead of her. Her only set plan was a meeting with Crispin the next day, meaning she had to make the most of her time with Fitz before then.

"What's your preference for staving off jet lag?" she asked, tone ebullient. "Stay up as long as possible, or straight to bed?"

The cabbie cleared his throat.

Fitz, gaze moving from her madly shaking leg to her face, reached out to take her hand, turning it over and tracing his thumb down the middle of her palm. "You're the boss."

Unlike her weeks on the Reach, this was *her*

arrangement. Unfortunately, the truth was she'd basically panicked and kidnapped the man, her plans beyond that hazy. And now, seeing him in his pea coat, in the back of a black cab, with familiar grey skies and hometown buildings flitting past the window, she could not help but picture a future in which that kind of thing happened, more. A lot. For forever.

Meaning she needed him to like it here, to love it here, more than ever.

"Sightsee?" she said.

Fitz nodded. "Show me what you got."

After dropping all their luggage with the concierge at Fitz's hotel near London Bridge, they decided to walk. While the Perth to London trip was truly unforgiving, the benefit of watching the city girl in her natural environment was too intriguing to forego.

It was a grey day in London—grey sky, grey river, grey buildings. Compared with the vivid scents of home, the air even tasted grey, yet it made the graphic pops of colour in the double-decker buses and signage advertising West End shows, and the vibrant flavours in the kebab she'd insisted they buy at the bustling Borough Market, all the richer.

Fitz drank it all in, relishing his first time away from Australia in years.

But mostly, he drank *her* in—her delight in showing off her city, and the confidence with which she navigated the streets and dealt with the noise and the crowds.

The chance to see Jackson had felt fortuitous. But the need to know if their connection, and how necessary she felt to him, existed outside of the heightened bubble in which they'd been living felt more imperative still.

He followed her on the tube to Westminster, ambling past Big Ben and Parliament, as she gave running history lessons. Until, when they hit Birdcage Walk, a long wide avenue taking them towards Buckingham Palace, she ran out of steam and the chatter faded.

Enjoying the smaller number of people and the colours of home in the piles of crisp leaves crunching under their feet, when they bumped shoulders, Fitz took his chance and curled her hand into his.

Mack glanced towards the touch, then up at him.

"Well, hello, there," he said.

Her brow furrowed. Then, she looked him in the eye, understanding washing over her. With a telling sigh, and a relieved huff of laughter, she slid her other hand into the crook of his elbow, and leaned her head against his arm.

"No more history lessons," she promised him.

"I like the history lessons. I just like being here with you more."

She looked at him, such keenness in her expression. "You do?"

Fitz glanced over his shoulder, then guided her towards a hedge by the park.

"I am well aware that you brought me here under false pretences, Ms. Lawler."

She swallowed. "I did."

"You were hoping I might take one look at the city and form the world's fastest case of Stockholm syndrome."

"I was."

Away from the pull of Kings Reach, the eddies of memory and meaning, the hunger for connection and continuity in a place that had taken as much as it had given, Fitz found the clarity he might never have been able to get a handle on there.

"In case it hasn't been made clear enough by the fact I just followed you across the world, I'm rather taken with you, Mack Lawler."

She coughed out a sob. "I had a feeling." Lifting up onto her toes and sliding her hands around his neck, she said, "So you are telling me this is real."

"Sure feels that way."

"What do we do now?"

Wrapping his arms about her, not loving the extra layers between them here, he said, "Earlier, you mentioned something about a bed?"

The surge of desire in her pretty hazel eyes had his gut twisting with need.

He leaned in and whispered against her ear, "Let's save your brother the cost of a hotel room."

"He can afford it," she whispered back, her eyes fluttering closed as he brushed kisses over her jaw.

Laughing through his need to get her out of her coat, Fitz said, "Ask me to stay with you, Mack."

"Stay with me," she said. "Stay with me forever."

Fitz felt a pinch of psychic pain in the back of his head; "forever" being a concept he'd excluded from his life a long time ago. There were too many variables, too many outside forces, too many ways things could go wrong no matter how tightly you held on.

But he was very much on board with giving Mack his now.

"Cab or tube?" he asked, sliding his lips over hers.

"Cab's quicker," she said, then yanking herself out of his grip, she ran to the curb and waved down a black cab that happened to be driving past, the yellow light atop switching off as it curved towards them.

And while Fitz did not believe in fate or any gods, he sent out thanks to whatever was watching over them in that moment.

Bags collected from the long-suffering concierge at the hotel, they turned off Holland Park Road, and under an archway reading Cottage Row Mews, beyond which came a row of neat white terraced homes, each behind wrought iron fences small enough to step over.

The black cab slowed, then zipped to cross into

oncoming traffic before pulling to a stop on the wrong side of the street.

"I'll never get used to that," Fitz mumbled.

Mack looked after payment then jogged up the steps to open the front door, leaving it wide for Fitz and the driver to bring in her multiple matching suitcases and Fitz's single battered leather satchel he'd picked up in Tijuana years before.

Then, alone in her foyer, the grey light of the day spilling over a black-and-white-checkered floor, a shabby but expensive-looking leather bench, several pairs of shoes tucked beneath, wall hooks filled with bags, and scarves and coats.

It was homey, eclectic, and warm. It was Mack.

"What do you think?" she asked, spinning around in the small space.

Fitz thought he'd spent twenty-four hours travelling, and another few walking a whole lot of streets that looked the same as the next. He also thought that wasn't why he'd come.

Fitz dumped his bag, kicked her front door shut, hauled her into his arms, and spun her about till she was pressed up against the wall.

Her breaths came hard; her eyes were diamond bright. And after a long moment in which they looked deep into one another's eyes, as if in challenge to see who would break first, Fitz lost.

Needing to feel her, he dragged her coat over her arms, letting the thing pool on the floor behind her. She did the same to him, tossing his coat on the bench.

"Unless you want me to find a hanger," she said, her voice hoarse as she kicked off her shoes and made to yank his jumper over his head at the same time. "I know you are a tidy guy."

Tidiness the very last thing on his mind, Fitz took her hands in his to slow her down. And after she stopped struggling, her wild gaze questioning, he separated her hands and placed them behind her, flat against the wall.

"Still," he said. And when she curled her fingers, pressing her hips forward, as if about to hurl herself at him, he took a step back.

"I'll stay," she promised.

Need turning his blood to lava, Fitz stepped in, using every ounce of self-control he had left to take his time. To pay attention. To make this special, for her.

Fingers still chilled from the London cold, he warmed them with his breath before undoing the top button of her starchy white shirt, then the next, and the next. Tugging the hem free of her jeans and sweeping the lapels aside, he took in the sweet white lace of her bra, the dark shadow of her nipples beneath.

With a growl, he slid his arm behind her and took one, bra and all, into his mouth. Good girl that she was, she kept her hands flat to the wall. Letting him kiss, and lick, and suck to his heart's content. She tasted of spun sugar and feminine heat, and the rough of the lace against his tongue was sweet torture.

When he pulled back to get his head on straight, he saw her shirt had fallen down her arms, trapping them at her sides. Her eyes were wild, her mouth open to catch as much breath as she was able. And in that moment forever didn't feel like long enough.

Once again shoving down the flicker of panic at the thought—the bigness of wanting always, for him, coming with the terror of losing—Fitz dropped to his knees, only to find the floor was rock-hard.

Spying a cushion on a chair down the hall, he got up, strode over, grabbed the thing, strode back, tossed it at Mack's feet and kneeled before her.

"You find this funny?" he asked, when she bit her lip to smother a laugh.

When he grabbed her by the belt loop and dragged her hip first, slowly, incrementally towards him, then placed a kiss just below her navel, her laughter became a ragged sigh.

Popping the button of her jeans and lowering the zip, he traced the edge of her white cotton underwear with his tongue. When she cried out, she bit her lip again.

"No need to be quiet for me," he instructed. "Make all the sounds you want."

Then he pulled her jeans down her lovely legs. Slowly, watching her face, as she writhed against the feeling of the fabric against her skin.

He tapped her feet, instructing her to step free, then took one ankle, positioning her feet wide.

Then wider again. Wide enough he saw the tremble in her legs. The anticipation turning her skin pink.

And when he nudged his nose against her sweet centre, she gasped. Loudly.

"Atta girl," Fitz murmured, shifting as the need between his own legs grew to an uncomfortable ache.

Then he tugged her underwear to one side and licked his way up in one long, slow move that nearly sent him over the edge. Enough was enough; he'd been wanting to do this, to have her, to please her, to ease her worry, for too long.

Reaching an arm around her backside, holding her to him, keeping her from collapsing as her legs shivered with need, he nuzzled, lathed, soothed, and suckled. Rhythmically, taking her more fully with every draw of his mouth. When her hands dropped to his head, holding him in place, he didn't stop her, instead lifting one of her legs over his shoulder, giving him the perfect path to what she wanted, what she needed.

And she began to quake—crying out his name, hands gripping his hair, hips moving against his mouth—until she stilled, breath caught in her lungs, before screaming out her pleasure so that the entire block might hear it.

Once the shivers rocking her body abated, he could feel the exhaustion overcoming her. From the time away, the flight home, the stresses she was under.

Kissing his way up her belly, her neck, he pulled himself to standing. There, he dragged the sleeves of her shirt back over her shoulders, and when he slid an arm beneath her knees and picked her up, she let him.

"Bedroom?" he murmured against her cheek.

"Upstairs," she managed.

Leaving their luggage for later, he carried her into her large bright bedroom, with its pretty green wallpaper and too many pillows, and after stripping her bare and laying her back on the bed, he found her bathroom, wet a wash cloth with warm water, and used it to wipe away the hours of travel.

Running it over her neck, her arms, her torso, till he reached between her legs.

By that stage, her skin had pinked in pleasure all over again, and her eyes were dark as she watched his ministrations. Watching her watch him, he pressed her legs apart, ran the soft wet fabric over her, gently then with thoroughness till she bucked and writhed beneath his touch.

Till reaching for him, pulling her to him, kissing him deeply, she came.

Minutes later, once he'd pulled the comforter over her naked body, he watched as her eyes drifted closed and she fell fast asleep.

His own exhaustion finally overcoming him, Fitz took a quick shower, where he took care of business in a shockingly quick amount of time. But that was Mack Lawler. She kept him on the verge at all times.

On the verge of desire, or frustration, or panic—it was a roll of the dice.

Done in, Fitz tossed the extra pillows to the floor and climbed into bed behind her, wrapping his arms about her sleeping body. She instantly turned to face him, wrapping herself about him and holding on.

Her eyes fluttered open, dopey with sleep. And seeing him she smiled, the deep affection in her eyes unmistakable. The meaning behind it splintering his heart.

And while that ought to have kept him up all night, trying to figure how the hell to manage it, slow it down, hold it at bay, he was fast asleep in seconds.

"So, what do you think?" Mack asked.

It was around three in the morning, London time, and she was lying in bed eating vanilla bean ice cream, a beautiful man on her pillow.

"About?" Fitz asked, his voice night rough, hot gaze on her mouth, twirling a finger through a lock of her hair over and over again.

"The city!"

"Honestly, I prefer Amsterdam. And Austin is right up there too."

Mack smacked him on the thigh, and his "oof" was half-hearted.

"Of course I have a soft spot for London," he said, his voice low.

Mack felt the sound skitter merrily through her veins.

Till he added: "I started my MBA at the London Business School."

Mack's spoon knocked against her teeth. "You've *lived* here before?"

"For a couple of months in my twenties."

"Why didn't you say something earlier?"

"You never asked."

What else had she not asked? So many things. Perhaps even a lifetime's worth.

"Why did you not finish?" *And stay, and bump into me on the street, and take one look at me and just know that we had magic between us?*

"My mother got sick. After the funeral, seeing how alone my father was, I decided to stay. Took the idea I had already been working on to open an ecotourism business, and transposed it there."

Mack leaned across him to put the empty ice cream tub on her bedside table, then rolled back to rest her hand on his chest, her chin on her hand. "Would you ever consider opening another, do you think? In the wilds of Britain, for example?"

Fitz's gaze traced the contours of her face before his eyes met hers. "Expansion has been mooted. But it won't be happening anytime soon. In fact, plans are afoot to double down back home."

Questions: No. *No questions.*

She knew he was the kind to jump on a horse to get where he needed to go, while she much preferred to book a driver. She loved the thrill of unearthing stories in the people around her, and while there were nine million of them in London, Fitz's nearest neighbour was a five-hour drive away. But she wanted to want him. Whatever happened from here, it was the best thing she had ever done for herself.

Mack wriggled herself to sitting, doing her best to ignore the heat in Fitz's eyes as the strap of her tank top dropped off her shoulder. Quickly moving it back into place, she said, "When we were on the plane, and sleep was proving impossible, I did some research."

"Does the woman never stop?" he said, curling a finger under the strap to make it fall once more.

"I read into twin-to-twin transfusion syndrome."

Fitz looked up.

"The way you described it," said Mack, before she lost her nerve, "you 'took too much blood' from Will. Well, I thought you should know that it's actually the opposite. Will was what they call the 'donor' twin, and the donor twin *donates* too much blood, which, yes, can lead to them being smaller, and have kidney issues, and suffer from anaemia. It wasn't your fault. It was never your fault."

Fitz looked at her as if her words were puzzle pieces scattered before him.

"It wasn't your fault," she repeated.

"I heard you," he said, a muscle ticking in his jaw.

She took his hand and shuffled in closer, her knees bumping up against his hip, as she said, "It was *not* your fault." Then, softly, one more time, "It was not your *fault*."

Slowly, then all at once, she saw her words sink in.

"Hell, Mack," he said.

"I know," she said, drawing him to her, leaning his head against her shoulder. And there she felt his big body shudder as he worked to forgive himself, allow softness inside of him—because she'd asked it of him.

And in his strength, she felt the words reflect back at her.

It wasn't her fault that her father hadn't acknowledged her.

It wasn't her fault Crispin had never really known what to do with her.

She blinked, and a tear slid down her cheek. Then another. Then another.

Then Fitz rolled her over, so that they became a tangle of sheets, and limbs, and breath, and touch.

"I want you, Mack," he said, whispering the words against her mouth. "I want this. To feel like this."

"I want it more," she assured him.

And they made love quietly, slowly, all attention and care. Before eventually falling asleep once more in one another's arms.

CHAPTER THIRTEEN

High above London, at the very best table in one of The Shard's most exclusive restaurants, Mack's fingers tripped over one another as she waited for Crispin to finalise his order.

She was keen to take the rare chance to talk, of course, but beneath it she was far more keen to get back to Fitz.

"So," Crispin said, as the wine he'd chosen breathed between them.

"So," Mack returned.

"Australia has done you good, yes?"

With Fitz's words tickling at the back of her mind, that her brother had sent her over there in order to help, not hinder her, she said, "I believe so."

"Good."

Just good? No mention of how he knew she had it in her? No offer of something juicy now she'd done as asked, and done it brilliantly? Mack shifted on her seat, the urge to…to get in her own way like a living thing inside of her.

But then Crispin pulled a file out of his suitcase,

opened it, and slid two stapled pieces of crisp A4 paper across the tablecloth.

Mack glanced down to see a printout of a draft article with *The Indicator* watermark, *The Indicator* heading, the title "Trouble in Paradise?" with her name alongside one of *The Indicator*'s most venerated journalists on the byline.

"What is this?" she asked, as the words and images jumbled in her attempt to read them.

"Draft of a piece we are planning to run. The seed of which was all yours, thanks to the file you insisted I look over."

Blinking, frantically, to clear her vision, panic crept into her throat at the phrases that jumped out at her. *Australian royalty. Family at odds. Changed wills. Unbreakable trust. Logan King legal challenge. Successful ecotourism business swept up in the maw.*

There were familiar snippets, to be sure. Questions she had jotted down after her numerous on-the-record interviews with Fitz, and chats with his family and staff. But the rest… Could it all be true? *If so, what a coup!* she thought, at near the very same time as thinking, *Oh, Fitz.*

Breathing deeply in order to somewhat settle her racing heart, she read it over a second time, and a third. All this, she mused, from notes she had offered up freely to Crispin. All this was due to the sharpness of her instincts, and the certainty there was more than met the eye when it came to the far-famed Outback family.

The truly sensational parts, though, had come from investigations made by *The Indicator* reporter, with mention of interviews with "sources close to the family" and public court records as lodged by Logan King, all of which revealed layers and intricacies Mack hadn't come close to being aware of. Layers that had been there for the taking, if only she'd looked harder. If only her feelings for Fitz hadn't, consistently, pulled her up short.

"How does it feel?" Crispin asked.

Mack looked up at her brother to find him smiling at her.

How did it *feel*?

How did it feel to recognise her words, her questions, attributed quotes from her collaborative file, appearing under *The Indicator* banner? Or how did it feel to know that Fitz had been dealing with *all of this* the entire time she had been getting to know him? That soon her family's paper would expose it all to the world, and her name would be on the byline.

It made her head hurt, her heart ache, her stomach tumble.

Only when she saw the smile on Crispin's face did it occur to her what he was really asking—how did it feel knowing that after all her hard work, her professional dream was about to come true?

She swallowed, her mouth dirt dry as she asked, "When is this going to print?"

"It is currently out for comment. Then, once legal has signed off, we'll run it."

Finally noting she wasn't turning cartwheels, he said, "Is there something you think we've missed? More we can add? It's 'Interest,' not 'Imperative,'" he said, referring to their internal Defcon levels, "so we can hold it a tad longer if you need more time to flesh it out."

Mack nodded, the thought of "more time" being the first thing about this whole conversation she could grab on to. For she had to show Fitz. Talk to Fitz. Let him know what was coming. Didn't she?

How that conversation would go, she had no clue. Would he understand? Possibly. Would he close ranks? Most definitely.

While her loyalty, such a marker of how she strove to move through the world, felt as if it was being torn in two.

"Can you…can you give me a day?" she asked.

Crispin nodded. "Certainly." Then, having poured wine in both glasses, he held his for a toast. "Welcome to *The Indicator*, Mackenzie, and to your first substantive byline. May it be the first of many."

Mack, on autopilot, lifted her glass and took the salute.

Though while she had envisaged this exact moment, manifested her little heart out for most of her life, she felt like she was watching it happen from behind a cracked mirror. For neither "a day" nor "all the time in the world" was enough time to figure out how to stop her world from falling apart one way or another.

* * *

Fitz whistled under his breath as he watched the numbers rise as the hotel lift took him to the penthouse of The Rochester, a seriously swanky boutique hotel in Mayfair—at once glad Jack had taken his call, *and* counting the time till Mack was done with lunch so he could take her back to bed.

While he'd booked a one-way ticket, his time there was limited. The Haven could run without him for a patch, but with wet season imminent, he needed to be available for the Reach too. Beyond that, he was already quietly working out a way to get back. Back to Mack.

For while he'd half convinced himself that in coming to London the bubble would pop, it had only expanded. He had expanded. Making him aware how distilled his life had become.

Fitz believed in the power of experiences. Hell, he sold them for a living. Yet he'd spent his life refusing to take part in the one that made the world go around. He'd preserved his emotions in the pain of how it felt to lose someone, without giving himself the chance to ever truly *have* someone in the first place.

But watching Mack at the luggage carousel at Heathrow, eyes bright as they watched the bags drop before shouting, "There!" when his old duffel had appeared, he'd known. He could be anywhere, at any time, going through anything, and she would be his gravity, his entertainment, his solace, and his light.

The lift pinged. When the doors opened Jackson strode across the private lobby, hand tucked into the pocket of his suit pants, tie a perfect knot, shoes spit shone.

"Hey, old man," said Fitz as he stepped from the lift.

"Hey, punk," the man rumbled, the ghost of an Australian accent haunting his deep English vowels.

Fitz glanced down at his chinos, pea coat, and navy knit, then looked up with a grin. "Mate, you've been hanging in fancy neighbourhoods for far too long. About time you come home and hang with some real tough guys."

At that Jackson laughed, a soft chortle that seemed to surprise even him. Then he swore beneath his breath, before reaching out and pulling Fitz into a tight hug.

Jackson took his time pouring them each a water from fancy bottles into fancy crystal cut glasses, before sliding one to Fitz, then taking a seat beside him at the kitchen bench.

The irony of their seating arrangement, the very King-ness of it all, was not lost on Fitz either, but he knew better than to say such a thing to Jack if he wanted to come away from this with some answers. And hopefully a fourth on #TeamBrothers, Tom's latest name for the group chat.

It would take some doing, he feared, taking in Jack's preternatural stillness, but there was enough familiarity in the way he lounged so like Tom, the elegance of movement so like Logan, and the colour of his eyes a dead ringer for their father. As well as the air of protectiveness he'd always given Fitz that no amount of distance or time seemed to exhaust.

"What brings you to sunny London?" Jackson asked.

"I'm actually here because of a woman," Fitz admitted. It felt both freeing and terrifying, as if saying it to any one of his brothers, the way they'd at one time talked about a crush, made it really real.

Jack's dark brows rose. "Anyone I know?"

Fitz opened his mouth to say it was unlikely, then remembered how he and Mack had first met. "Possibly. She's a Londoner. Mackenzie Lawler. She writes for *The Pulse*."

Jack's response was visceral—he reared back, a muscle ticking in his jaw, then he pushed back his chair and strode from the room. A minute later he returned with a yellow envelope and handed it to Fitz. "Then maybe you can tell me what the hell this is all about."

A zing of trepidation scooted down Fitz's spine, like the first crackle in the air heralding an impending spring storm. Fingers feeling too big for his hands, he pulled a sheaf of papers from the envelope.

The top was a cover letter, on *The Indicator* letterhead, requesting comment. The next two pages, stapled together, were the draft of an article entitled "Trouble in Paradise?" written by Trinity Jones and…

And Mackenzie Lawler.

And for the first time in over a decade, after all the work he'd put in to make sure it never, ever happened again, Fitz was wholly unprepared as he felt the bottom drop out of his life.

Mack's stomach dropped faster than the lift taking her down into the belly of The Shard, and in an effort to keep from heaving, she rolled her phone over and over in her hand, hoping some answer might come to her as to what on earth she was meant to do.

Seeing her name on *The Indicator* byline was proof that her talent was hard-won. Proof she'd finally been *noticed*, *seen* for her skills, and not the name she'd never asked for. But the repercussions of such a story going live tumbled over her like a rockslide.

If Fitz's father *had* made such a decision, it would pit his sons against one another, and most certainly against him, and definitely put Hideaway Haven in danger. Not that she doubted any point in the article, for *The Indicator* writers and researchers always did their due diligence; it's why they were the literal best. It was just a most dire situation for people she…she had come to care for.

The lift doors opened, and she slipped through the crowd, out the doors, and into the dreary day.

And there, in the building's forecourt just across

the way, stood a man in a navy pea coat, navy knit, and chinos, hands shoved deep into his pockets, looking up at the façade. A man who made her heart lift so she had to draw breath.

"Fitz!" she called, her voice breaking just a little, only to have to pause as a red double-decker bus slowly crawled around the curved street separating her from the other side.

When the bus passed, Fitz had turned, and by the hard look in his eyes, the set of his stubbled jaw, even before she saw a yellow envelope rolled up in his hand, a matching one to the one Crispin had given her, she knew.

Fitz knew about the article. He knew it contained information he and his staff had offered up to her freely, not knowing how easily it might lead to deeper truths. And he knew her name was on the byline.

She also saw, in his eyes, that it was all true. That his father's plans had been sitting heavily on him for months. Not that he'd shared any of that with her—either because he'd not seen her as the person with whom to share his most difficult days as much as she'd thought he had, or because deep down he knew not to trust her. Or both.

Heart aching, heart *breaking*, Mack steeled herself and crossed the street.

When Fitz took a few steps her way, she felt a flicker of hope, but then he stopped, leaving more distance between them than he ever had.

"This feels terribly like pistols at dawn," she

said, in an attempt at levity. Hoping they could find a path back to the bubble they'd been living in, a place of sharing, and comfort, and intimacy the likes of which she'd never known.

Then Fitz held up the envelope with *The Indicator* logo stamped on the corner, the thing curled so tightly in his hand it all but bent in half.

"Where did you get that?" she asked, voice croaking.

"Jackson."

Of course. It had been sent out for comment. And Crispin wouldn't have imagined he could find Fitz at hers.

"What the hell, Mack?"

She held out both hands, in supplication. "It's not what you think—"

"It's *not* an article laying out intimate details of an extremely private family matter, the release of which may have devastating repercussions not just for myself, and my business, but our staff, and my family, and…and the Australian beef industry—"

Mack blinked. "Okay," she said, when his anguish became unbearable. "Yes. It is all those things. Only *I* did not write it."

Something flickered over his face then. Hope? Belief? Certainty she was in his corner? All of which was absolutely fair, because she loved him.

She loved him. So of course she was in his corner. Just as he had been in hers. If working for *The Indicator* had been a dream, that kind of connection with someone had been a longing so deep she'd all but given up on it. Until Fitz King had slammed into her life.

What a moment to realise such a momentous thing!

Only, right as she felt the happiness and joy and delight and wonder that came with knowing one was in love for the first time in one's life—Fitz's expression grew stoic.

And yet he took another step her way. "If you didn't write it, why does it say that you did?"

She held his gaze as she said, "Because they used my notes, and my research, as the bones of the story, then other writers and researchers found the rest from there."

Fitz's hands fell open in question, his face twisting in disbelief.

Only she wasn't sure what else she could say, for it was the truth. And she had done nothing wrong. She had been doing her job.

Falling in love with him had been the mistake. No, not the mistake, the...the spanner in the works, the monkey in the wrench, the complication she simply did not know how to command.

"Look," he said, moving closer and holding out a hand as if he still might be able to grab hold of the tail of the magic that had glimmered over them. "Can you at least give me an assurance that you can put a stop to this?"

His gaze roved over her face as if he'd find all the truth he'd ever need, right there.

But she was on a merry-go-round of feelings

and words. *Trust, inclusion, byline, future, earned it, want more, dreams, love.* There were just too many coming at her, and no time to put them into separate silos so she could deal with each individually. So, she said the first thing that came to mind.

"Is it true?" she asked.

Fitz reared back as if she'd taken a swing at him.

"Is it true?" she asked again, softening her voice this time. "Because if it is, and if every source spoke on the record, and if it is in the public interest..." Which, considering the players, and the land at stake, there was no denying it was. "There is nothing to be done. For if the Lawler papers don't run it, soon enough, someone else will."

Fitz ran a hand through his hair, looking at her in that moment, as if he didn't really know her at all. Only he did. He knew that truth was important to her. He knew she'd never hurt him or his family if she had a choice. But she understood, completely, why that might not matter. Not now, and maybe not ever. For him, as for her, family was the greatest leveller of all.

A light mist began to fall, then, suddenly, dumping rain. Mack, only just realising that in her fugue must have left her coat in the cloakroom after lunch, shivered as the damp seeped into her clothes.

Despite Fitz's patent pain and confusion, he whipped off his coat as he went to her. Holding it over her head, he hauled her against him as together they ran towards The News Building. There, after quickly charming the security guards into letting them duck under the awning, he shook out his coat before putting it over Mack's shoulders. Wrapping her in his warmth, his scent. She drank it all in, the way one might take a final glass of water before walking into the desert.

Fitz reached out to fix the coat's collar. His fingers brushed her neck, and it shook something free in him. Shaking his head, he ran his fingers down the lapels and gripped them tightly as he stepped in closer—an anchor, holding on to all that had felt so possible only hours before.

His brow was deeply lined, his jaw hard as he said, "Hell, Mack. Just…hell."

Mack lifted her shoulders in agreement. And her mind spun with memory of the laughter and intimacy they'd shared, curled up in her bed that morning. The kiss behind the waterfall. His heartbreaking confessions by the fire. Her own tales of loneliness and sorrow that she had told to him.

She held his gaze, hoping he'd see how much every second she'd spent with him meant to her. How much she wished she *had* done something wrong so there was something to undo.

Then Fitz said, "I have to go. I have to talk to my family. Warn them. Fix this, somehow. Dammit, Mack, I was so ready…" His gaze dropped to her mouth, and after a hot, soulful beat, his eyes clouded so that she could no longer see even a hint of warmth therein. "I should have seen this coming. This mess was definitely my fault."

And with that, he held his arm over his face and ran out into the rain.

Shaking despite Fitz's body warmth still clinging to his coat, Mack watched him disappear into the mist.

And while the urge to call his name swelled within her, she bit it back. She'd been rebuffed, left on the outer, and overlooked too many times in her life to welcome it by choice. She would not beg him to believe her, or forgive her, or even to understand her.

All she could do, all she'd ever done, was hold tight to her own truth. For at the end of the day, if no one else chose her, she simply had to choose herself.

CHAPTER FOURTEEN

SINCE HE COULD hardly go back to Mack's place, Fitz sat in some bar near London Bridge nursing a drink he'd left untouched for so long the ice had melted. Shivering on occasion, having given up his coat and not quite dried out as yet. The crumpled yellow envelope with *The Indicator* insignia lay twisted at his elbow.

He'd taken photos of the pages and sent them to Tom and to Logan, in case they'd not been contacted for comment as yet. After a beat he'd also sent them to Ned and to Julian, as they deserved a heads up as to what might be coming at them. His partners in all but name in this venture, he'd left them in the dark for far too long.

At the last he sent it to his father. Then he turned his phone to silent and put it away.

Drink twisting beneath his hand, Fitz's mind went straight to Mack. The fact that she was involved in this mess, and refused to make it go away, didn't mean he could turn that off.

Hell, that morning they'd made love, looking

into one another's eyes, whispering plans and promises. *I want you. I want this. I want it more.*

Even while he'd been stunned stupid after reading the article, mind reeling with all the ways he wanted to be angry with her, when he'd seen her on the other side of the street, striding towards him, looking like a vision in her starched white shirt tucked into tweed pants, high heels clacking on the bitumen, dark hair flicking in the misty breeze, he'd felt as if his heart was about to leap from his chest.

Fitz ran his hand over his face. Then took a swig of the drink, only to wince at the watered-down nothingness. He slid it back across the bar. Then took the papers from the crushed envelope and read them again.

It was all there—his father's announcement at the ball, Logan's legal attempts to stop him, Tom working from the Reach for a few months in the hopes of changing their father's mind, Fraser's knee injury and growing frailty, whispers of shifting foundations among staff at the Reach.

Mack said she hadn't written it, so even if the voice didn't read like her—too dry, too quietly judgemental—he'd have believed her. But her notes had been the seed, without which he'd not be sitting there.

And yet, as he read it over again, he noticed there were a multitude of things that were also not in the article. There was nothing about his mother, and there was nothing about Will. There was no hint about any animosity arising from his brothers blaming his father for Will's death.

Fitz could have sworn the times they'd spoken of all that he'd not invoked off-the-record status, and yet while she had been thorough in other areas, she must have left those conversations out of her notes completely.

She'd chosen not to jot down spice that could have sold papers by the bucketload, the kind that would help her really make a name for herself—

Before he could finish that thought, a body slid into the chair beside his, and Fitz turned to find Jackson brushing water droplets from his coat as if they were grime.

"Hello?" said Fitz. "How the hell did you find me here? Unless..." He clicked his fingers. "You're the ghost of Christmas past."

"That group chat you lot are all suddenly so fond of has a GPS tracker."

"So, you won't speak to us, or visit us, but you watch where we go on some app?"

Jackson lifted a single eyebrow, as if it mattered not a jot. But to Fitz it meant that while his oldest brother refused to take part in any King family bunkum, he did not *not* care. Which left the smallest flicker of hope that if they couldn't stop Fraser from breaking the trust, at least the guy might not "burn the whole place to the ground."

"So, what's the plan?" asked Jackson, glancing at the papers.

"I hoped you might have some crack legal team breathing fire in their general direction by now."

"Not sure what makes you think I would suddenly involve myself. And, unless you tell me otherwise, I assume it is all true."

Fitz leaned his elbows on the bar and his head in his hands.

"This was coming," Jackson said. "The truth will come out, it always does. My advice—stop overthinking. Figure out what's making you mad, and either let it go or fix it. Anything else is a waste of time."

Then Jackson stood, threw some cash on the bar, gave Fitz's shoulder a squeeze, tossed the coat he must have taken off while Fitz sat their moping over Fitz's back, and was gone.

Fitz lifted his head and slid his arms into the thing, catching pieces of his reflection between the bottles in front of the mirror behind the bar. What was making him mad?

Mack, he thought. *Mack has made me mad.* Only as soon as he thought the words, he knew that it wasn't true.

For all that he'd told himself what a huge step it was following Mack to London, he'd been holding his breath the entire time. Waiting for her to change her mind, or realise he wasn't all she imagined him to be. Certain he would lose her somehow.

Reading that article had been a relief.

There was the piano he'd been waiting to fall

upon his head. Finally, he had an excuse to pull away before he fell any deeper. When he went home, he could stop waking in the middle of the night reaching for her, sweating bullets till he remembered she was safe and sound.

Not that he'd told her any of that when they'd found one another.

Fitz wasn't sitting at that bar feeling angry with Mack, he was furious with himself.

And now, after earning the thing she'd always wanted, Mack was out there somewhere, torn up inside. And having spent her life feeling as if no one had her back, he'd left her to go through it alone.

Fitz rubbed both hands over his face in an effort to scrub his mind clean.

Blame is a nasty witch.

He'd spent years blaming himself or an ill-thought-out conversation he'd had as a nine-year-old kid. Because he was born tough and Will was not. Blaming himself for any time anyone gave Will grief, or picked on him for being quiet or small. Because he'd been born big and hot-headed and Will had not.

When the truth was, he and Will had been the best of friends, playing card games in the treehouse, building Lego together every Christmas, naming the feral cats, for that had been a team effort after all. He missed the kid, so damn much.

But if he spent the rest of his life looking for blame, owning the blame, carrying the weight of his family on his back all alone, it would not be much of a life. Not when compared with the vivid, challenging, delectable days he's spent with Mack.

Mack, knowing him like nobody else, seeing him like no one ever would, had held his hand, looked him in the eye, and told him it was not his fault.

Now it was his turn to do the same for her.

And if she refused to hear him, at least he would be able to look anyone in the eye, including himself, and know he'd done his all to win her back.

Mack and Priya sat in one of the meeting rooms in *The Pulse* offices, looking out over the view of the Tower of London.

Priya sipped slowly at her can of soda, using a bunch of different reusable straws she was reviewing for a *The Pulse* piece Alicia had okayed for her to write, while Mack's tea went cold.

"Have I said I'm sorry?" Priya asked.

"Seventy-twelve times," said Mack, giving her friend a smile. "Even though you did nothing wrong."

And after spending all afternoon and evening checking and rechecking her notes to make sure her collaboration file was clean and only contained attributed notes, Mack was 100 percent certain she hadn't either.

If anything, she'd held back, put the subject before the story. And while in the past she'd have been mortified with herself for making such a choice, with time and space and a heck of a lot of navel gazing, she knew that this time it sat with her just fine.

For Crispin had been right all along: *The Indicator* was not the home for her.

That was one of the reasons she'd asked her brother to take her name off the story. Yes, it was all above board, but it did not sit well with her conscience. She simply did not have the required killer instinct. And that was actually okay.

The other reason came down to love. And while her heart felt as if it had been pummelled with a meat tenderiser, she was okay with that too.

She loved, and had been loved. She was certain of it. And while she'd messed things up wholesale, it was a truth that could not be taken away.

Mack glanced out at *The Pulse* offices with the plethora of bright white quarter cubicles, desks covered in framed photos and potted plants. The publication wall covered ceiling to floor in coloured Post-it notes showing the stories people were currently working on.

Compared to the sombre offices of *The Indicator*, the place screamed fun and innovation, and she felt a not too subtle glimmer of guilt at how badly she'd taken it for granted. It was nearing nine in the evening and there were a dozen writers still at work. Some were dolled up, about to head to a movie premiere after-party, a few were sharing a bowl of crisps, huddled over someone's phone as they played some new viral dance video. And she knew it was by choice, not duty.

It would be around five in the morning at Kings Reach, the station hands would be saddled up, chasing the early light to avoid the worst heat of the day. She knew not just because she'd asked, but because her curiosity had extended beyond the luxury of the Haven to the dirt, and flies, and sweat, and rich history of the station proper. All of which she hoped Fitz and his family could keep secure.

And while windmills might be her nemesis for evermore, the realisation that she'd never be invited back there again was a deep cut.

Not once had delivering a story early, or under word count, made her feel happier than she'd felt waking up to those golden sunrises, the field of rainbow lorikeets feeding on the ground outside her cabin, the whisper of warm earthy air on her skin. Knowing she'd see Fitz King at some point that day, even if she had to hunt him down herself.

The realisation she may never see Fitz King again…

She couldn't go there, not yet. In fact, she might not ever be able to go home again either, in case when he'd gone he'd left something of himself behind. Oh, who was she kidding, what did stuff matter, when the man had imprinted himself on her heart and soul?

"Should I stay?" Mack asked, when what she really wanted to know was *could* she.

"At *The Pulse*?" Priya asked, perking up.

Mack leaned over and squeezed her knee. "In London. If the past weeks have taught me anything it's that I need to get out more."

Mack watched in surprise as literal tears gathered in Priya's eyes. She dragged her chair over to Priya's and pulled her into a hug. "You will be fine! Look at you, writing your first byline. Swings and roundabouts, my love."

Priya smiled, then, looking over Mack's shoulder, her mouth dropped open in shock. "Oh, my gods, that's him."

"Him who?" Mack turned and followed Priya's eyeline to find Fitz King cutting a striking figure in a knee-length coat—for she had his pea coat still—striding through *The Pulse* offices, scooting around the space between desks, a wave of sighs and swoons following in his wake.

And no wonder—even without the cowboy hat and the riding boots, he had a swagger and an earthy, primal, that-man-can-toss-me-over-his-shoulder-and-not-break-a-sweat vibe that even now, with questions galore dancing about inside her head, made Mack's knees tingle.

Around halfway, he stopped, asked one of the women in a party dress a question, and after quickly fixing her hair, she turned and pointed right at Mack.

Fitz's gaze shifted, found hers, and even beneath the bright fluorescent lights, the intensity in the man's steel-blue gaze was patent. And Mack could no longer feel her toes.

She somehow managed to stand, ran hands down the sides of her tweed pants, and walked on unsteady legs out of the meeting room. He moved through the desks and she did the same till they stopped a couple of metres away from one another.

"Hi," she said, her voice utterly breathless. "How did you get in here? Security in this place is second to none."

"I called your brother."

"Crispin? Why on earth—"

"To give him my comments on the story."

"The story?" she asked, fully aware that she was not coming up with the best words possible, but how could she when Fitz was *there*?

"You know what he told me?"

Mack had a fair idea.

"He told me you no longer work here anymore."

Oh. That.

For not only had Mack asked for her name to be taken off the story, she'd handed in her resignation. Effective immediately.

If Crispin had gone silent when she'd asked him to take her name off the story, she'd worried he'd had a heart attack when she'd quit.

"What will you do?" he'd finally asked after a long pause, as if life outside of the Lawler Media Group was a veritable wasteland.

"Not sure yet. Maybe I'll write for the competition."

Expecting another bout of apoplexy, instead her brother had laughed. "Good for you, kid. Sincerely.

I thought about getting the hell out of here more times than I can remember when I was your age, but I never had the guts. I know it might not help, considering we're family, but you'll have a glowing reference in your email first thing tomorrow."

Family. He'd called her his family. To think that all it had taken was for her to take a risk, fail, get in trouble, be sent away, come back, and refuse to take the offer he'd made and quit.

"Please tell me you did not give up your job because of the story…because of me," said Fitz, his voice low now, just enough to reach her and no one else.

"I quit because of me." Mack lifted her shoulders in a mini-shrug, when all she wanted to do was run into his arms, and hold him, and have him hold her. "I thought you'd be long gone."

"Not yet," he rumbled. "Things to do here first."

And when his gaze met hers, she knew. There was hope. There was belief. There was certainty they were in one another's corners. Still.

Close enough to reach for her, he did just that, right as she reached for him. With her hands cupping his elbows, as his hands ran up and down her arms, it reminded her of the night they'd first met, in the centre of his family's fancy barn, her purse filled with stolen chocolates.

"Your family must hate me right now," she said, her voice hoarse with emotion.

"Nah," he said. "For all our attempts at self-sabotage, when push comes to shove, we fight back-to-back when it comes to protecting our own."

Mack might have sobbed. Or maybe it was a laugh. There was no telling with the amount of emotion rushing through her.

Though she did recognise the twittering and sighing coming from the other side of the space, as their audience bunched together to watch the unusual goings on. Uncurling Fitz's hand from her arm, Mack used it to tug him behind her. His hand in hers felt so right, so warm and strong, her heart stuttered madly against her ribs.

Priya, seeing them coming, beckoned them into the meeting room, then bowed as if Fitz was an actual prince, before leaving and shutting the door behind them. Then she flapped her arms at their audience and shooed them all away.

Hand still cocooned in his, Mack drew Fitz deeper into the room, till they reached the corner by the window, the lights of London catching in his eyes.

And there, Fitz lifted his hand to capture her chin, his thumb pressing gently to her bottom lip. "My father," he said, his gaze roving over her face, "at the end of the Eliza King Foundation Ball, told my brothers and I that he had started proceedings to break the irrevocable trust."

Mack put her hands over her ears. "Stop. Stop talking. Or tell me this is off the record."

"He has plans to make my older brother Jackson the sole voice of management, which means he would be able to do whatever he pleased with the place. Tom, Logan, and I have been working together to stop it, while Jackson… We don't know what Jackson's plans might be." Fitz breathed out long and slow. "And that's all of it."

Dropping her hands, her voice was a whisper as she said, "Why are you telling me this now?"

"Because I want you to know everything there is to know about me. No secrets, no bumps in the night. I'm sure I'll miss things, forget things, but I'll never keep anything from you ever again."

Fitz's mouth lifted at the corners, his eyes roving over her face as if he knew how close they'd come to him never having the chance to do so again.

Gaze darkening, voice dropping, he ran his thumb back and forth across the dip below her mouth as he stepped in closer.

"So," he said, "what's the plan?"

"The plan?" she managed, her skin feeling feverish as his hot body pressed her into the corner.

"Now you're out of work. If you're looking for a job, we're always after stations hands at Kings Reach."

Mack laughed, her gaze catching on his. "I think we can both agree my skills lie elsewhere."

"Mmm," Fitz said, leaning down to rumble against her ear. "Either way, what do you say to leaving this ridiculous weather behind for some fresh air and sunshine, just for a little while, so together we can work on those skills? See what we can add to your résumé, while you figure out what to do next."

"Fitz," she said, knees giving way as she grabbed the lapels of his coat.

"All of which is a ham-fisted way of saying, come home with me, Mack. Be with me. I should have asked long before this but I've lost a lot of people in my life, and it's made it hard to trust that anyone I love might actually stay."

Mack swallowed. Had he just intimated—

"Let me be plain and simple. I love you, Mack. And if you can't stay, I'll follow. Whenever I can. If you'll let me. Because the thought of living my life without you in it makes no sense to me at all."

Mack didn't realise a tear had spilled down her cheek till Fitz swiped it with his thumb. Then followed with a string of kisses down her cheek till his lips pressed to her mouth.

Senses spinning like a pinwheel, all dizzying colour and joy, Mack opened his coat and she slid her hands around his waist, absorbing all that glorious body heat till she felt all melty. And wonderful. And as if she'd woken to find herself in a dream.

And while getting the heck out of there and dragging the man back to her bed felt imperative, there were still things to say.

"You love me," she said, unable to curb the sparkles in her voice.

"Turns out, I do," he said on a chortle of warm laughter.

"I just wanted to fact-check. Make sure I didn't misquote you."

When she left it at that, Fitz's growl nearly took her under. Only so many words were piling up at the back of her tongue she had to let them free.

She lifted her head and looked into his eyes. "You do know I love you too, right?"

His breath out was pure relief. The big galumph.

"I love you so much, I can barely stand it. I love that you read old Westerns and can watch *Pride and Prejudice* unironically. I love how you go barefoot as often as you can and that you have strong opinions about toasted marshmallow choices. I love how deeply you think, how protective you are of those under your care, and how you love where you come from so much you've made it your mission to encourage others to love it too."

"Thank the stars," he said on a bark of rough laughter when she stopped to take a breath.

Letting out a huge happy sigh, Mack said, "I'd be thrilled to come share your fresh air and sunshine for as long as I'm able."

"And I'll follow wherever you need to be."

"We are really doing this?" she asked, astonished that this was all happening to her.

"I've spent my entire life keeping people at arm's length out of fear of losing them. I don't want to lose a minute more now of knowing you."

Was it possible for a person's heart to break and mend all in one go?

Sliding her hand up his front, Mack gripped his

jumper in her fist and gave it a light shake. "I hope you know that's a testament to your great big heart how many people you have collected who love you while actively trying not to."

"So long as I have one," he said, "and that the one is you, then I'm golden."

"And supposedly I'm the wordsmith."

"You and me," said Fitz, settling against her. "What do you say?"

"You and me," she agreed on a sigh.

Then, shaking his head as if in wonder, Fitz moved his spare hand to rest it against the wall by her head as he leaned into her, his mouth hovering an inch from hers, and a muffled scream came through the glass.

Mack bit her lip so as not to laugh, while Fitz's steel-blue eyes danced.

"We have an audience still, don't we?" he asked.

Mack looked over Fitz's shoulder to find a half-dozen women huddled together on the other side of the door. When they saw her spy them, they panicked, banged into one another, and fled in several directions.

When her gaze moved back to his she knew he'd never stopped looking at her. Because he loved her. And he saw her. And wanted a life with her.

"What now?" she asked.

"Now this." Fitz leaned down to nudge her nose with his, to lay a row of soft kisses along her cheek, his stubble sending shooting sparks all over her body.

Then with a rumbled promise, filthy and fabulous, that shocked through her like lightning, he covered her mouth with his.

EPILOGUE

One month later...

THE BIG WET was coming; Fitz could smell it on the air.

Add the eerie lack of birdsong, the rise in goanna sightings near the house, and the number of ant mounds they'd come across on the ride that morning, wild and woolly times were ahead for Kings Reach. That, and a dramatic slowing of the bookings Hideaway Haven would accept for the safety of their guests, despite the astronomical influx of interest that Mack's beautiful, sensitive, measured, final *The Pulse* article had brought on.

Yini snickered as Mack's horse, Amanpour—a gentle-footed light grey mare they'd picked out for her at stock sales after returning from London—walked a little close. Fitz ran a stilling hand down the edgy gelding's neck.

In a white shirt, cream jodhpurs, and her brand-new, sand-coloured Akubra—for the woman had no fear of red dirt—Mack looked like she'd stepped off a movie set, rather than dressing beside the bed while he'd watched after waking early enough to indulge in some bedroom fun that morning,

"How's that gorgeous backside of yours?" Fitz asked, heat rushing through him at her upright gait atop her lightly prancing pony.

Mack shot him a look.

He laughed. "You'll get there. I have every faith."

They were nearing the end of Mack's first muster. Only a single paddock day, as the whole station muster, requiring stockmen, horses, helicopters, ATVs, drones, and working dogs moving a million head in readiness for the coming rains, would take weeks.

The next day Fitz and Mack were heading back to London for a spell, as after taking a couple of weeks off, the downtime sending her around the bend, she'd landed a column writing features for a site nipping at *The Pulse*'s popular heels. As *Girl About Town*, she'd already banked stories on a few of the station staff. She was working on Annalise, with no luck yet.

Ned, Julian, and a skeleton non-seasonal crew would stay on to look after the crazy adventurer types who chose to stay at the Haven at that time of year on purpose. As Ned and Julian had been the ones to okay the article that lead to their email inbox ticking over with hundreds of enquiries a day, they'd be earning their keep as freshly minted partners, having officially bought into the Hideaway Haven business.

With Kings Reach also now owning a 10 percent share, tying the businesses together, rain or shine, and giving the Haven a financial kick that meant they could truly look into expansion, there was plenty of work to go around.

"Hey, you pair."

Fitz glanced to his left, where his father walked Emperor, his giant of a mount. "Dad," he said, with a nod.

"Fences checked?"

"Check."

Since his return from London, and since the new deal between the Reach and the Haven had been signed off, Fitz was now explicitly included in all such upper management decisions on the station. And so far, it was working out just fine.

Perry, the Kings Reach station manager, joined them on Fraser's other side. "Pumps have been raised, generators all above last year's flood level."

"I'll get onto the gutters this afternoon," Fitz added. It would be his last job before he and Mack were off.

"Good stuff," said Fraser. Then, smiling at Mack, he asked, "How's she working out for you?" Fraser had turned up to the stock sale, and when he'd shown interest in Mack's thought process, Fitz had hung back, let Fraser and Mack work together to pick the right mount. They'd been enamoured of one another ever since.

"Oh, I adore her." Mack lifted the tip of her hat

to gift his father the kind of smile that made the man colour, just a little, every time.

"Glad to hear it." Then, "Alrighty. Let's move on out," Fraser called out, voice carrying across to the dozen other riders out with them that day, and with a click of the tongue and a nudge of a boot he and his horse took off to join the crew.

"Excited to be heading home?" Fitz asked.

Mack, who had been looking out across the acres of cracked sun-bleached land, grass yellowed and laid flat from months of dryness, the distant hills melting into the skyline in the glinting heat, said the words that would remind him, again and again over the years, how lucky he was to have found her.

"We are home."

Running a hand over Yini's mane, Fitz edged his horse close enough to hers to lean in and kiss her shoulder.

Mack lifted her hand to his neck and drew him in for a quick hard kiss, before nudging her mare to a canter—the homestead in sight, the rest of their lives a brilliant promise awaiting them beyond the shimmering horizon.

* * * * *

Look out for the next story
in Outback Kings quartet
Stuck with Her Impossible Ex
by Kandy Shepherd

And if you enjoyed this story, check out
these other great reads from Ally Blake

Fake Dating the Italian Heir
Dating Deal with the Italian
Always the Bridesmaid

All available now!